Hank quickly assessed his options, knowing if he told Colette yes, she'd want to know the details. It was better she not know. Not remembering those details just might save her life.

He looked at the baby in the crib, recalled cradling her little body in his arms. "No," he answered, then balling his hands into fists, he turned and left.

Colette watched him go, the murmur of fear dancing inside her. Who was Hank Cooper, and why did he affect her so strongly? She had the distinct feeling he'd lied, that she did know him from someplace other than this ranch.

Why would he lie about knowing her? What had he been in her past? And why was he so interested in her baby?

She picked up her infant, needing to hold her close, assure herself of the child's safety. She walked to the window. Staring out, she remembered the nightmare that had plagued her the night before. The eyes she'd dreamed of, she now realized, had been Hank's eyes.

SAFE HAVEN

CARLA CASSIDY

Sunset Promises

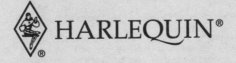

HARLEQUIN®

TORONTO • NEW YORK • LONDON
AMSTERDAM • PARIS • SYDNEY • HAMBURG
STOCKHOLM • ATHENS • TOKYO • MILAN • MADRID
PRAGUE • WARSAW • BUDAPEST • AUCKLAND

ISBN-13: 978-0-373-36205-9
ISBN-10: 0-373-36205-6

SUNSET PROMISES

Copyright © 1997 by Carla Bracale

This edition published by arrangement with Harlequin Books S.A.

® and TM are trademarks of Harlequin Books S.A., used under license. Trademarks indicated with ® are registered in the United States Patent and Trademark Office, the Canadian Trade Marks Office and in other countries.

www.eHarlequin.com

Printed in U.S.A.

CARLA CASSIDY

Carla Cassidy is an award-winning author who has written more than fifty novels for Silhouette Books. In 1995, she won the Best Silhouette Romance award from *Romantic Times BOOKreviews* for her novel *Anything for Danny*. In 1998, she also won a Career Achievement Award for Best Innovative Series from *Romantic Times BOOKreviews*.

Carla believes the only thing better than curling up with a good book to read is sitting down at the computer with a good story to write. She's looking forward to writing many more books and bringing hours of pleasure to readers.

Prologue

Moonlight filtered through the leaves of the ancient oak tree, shining silvery shards of light onto the three girls seated directly beneath its gnarled, misshapen branches.

For as long as the girls could remember, the tree had been referred to as the dragon tree. Their mother had told them the tree had been struck by lightning dozens of times, resulting in blackened twisted branches and dense foliage that through the spring and summer grew in the shape of a dragon. In the autumn, the magnificent beast appeared to shed fire-colored scales.

Rather than be frightened, the three girls had embraced the tree, fitting it into their childhood fantasies of princes and castles, of princesses and love. And the words, "the dragon tree," had become their secret code…a phrase that always resulted in a late night meeting at its foot.

"What's going on?" Colette, the youngest of the three, looked expectantly at her two other sisters. At twelve, Colette possessed the impatience of a newborn colt trying to stand. She leaned against the trunk of the tree, slivers of moonbeams highlighting her youthful features.

"Yeah, Abby. What's going on? Why'd you call us here?" Belinda asked. At thirteen years old, Belinda was the middle sister, often the peacemaker between the slightly spoiled Colette and the often controlling Abby.

Fifteen-year-old Abby wrapped her arms around her knees and rocked back and forth, the moonlight caressing her straight nose and the strong thrust of her jaw. "I found some papers today in Mom's dresser drawer."

"What kind of papers?" Belinda asked.

Abby looked first at Belinda, then at Colette. "Adoption papers."

The words hung in the air, seemingly isolated from the other sounds of the night. Although they had been whispered, they resounded louder than the lowing of the cattle in the distance, more pronounced than the high-pitched neigh of a horse from the nearby corral and much more frightening than the eerie echoing howl of a coyote in the hills.

"Adoption papers?" Belinda finally broke the silence. "Adoption papers for who?"

"I didn't look." Abby pulled a hand through her short blond hair. "It was just a manila envelope and written on it was 'adoption papers.' I saw it, then heard Mom coming down the hall so I didn't get a chance to open it. I went back in later to look, but the papers weren't there anymore."

"But...but that means one of us must be..."

"No," Colette interrupted. "No, I don't want to hear about it, I don't even want to think about it."

She leaned forward and reached for Abby's hand, then grabbed Belinda's, as well. "We're sisters. The three of us and no stupid papers will ever change that."

"Belinda? Do you feel the same way about it?" Abby asked.

Belinda squeezed both her sisters' hands. "Of course. I don't ever want to know which one of us might be in that folder."

Abby withdrew her hands and reached into her pocket. "I was hoping you guys would say that." She pulled out a large safety pin. "I vote we become blood sisters and we vow we'll never try to find out which one of us might be adopted." She opened the wicked-looking pin, the sharp point gleaming in the moonlight. Colette and Belinda watched as she pricked her skin. As the blood welled up on her fingertip, she handed the pin to Belinda, who did the same and passed the pin to Colette.

Colette frowned, her bottom lip caught between her teeth. "Do it for me, Belinda," she said, holding out her finger and squeezing her eyes tightly closed.

A squeal escaped her at the sharp sting of the puncture. She opened her eyes, keeping her gaze on her sisters and averted from the blood.

"Sisters forever," Abby proclaimed solemnly, holding her finger toward them.

"Sisters forever," Belinda echoed, pressing her finger against Abby's.

"And no matter what happens, we never read those stupid papers," Colette exclaimed. She waited for Abby and Belinda to nod their heads in agreement, then added her finger to theirs, forming a triangle of unity.

With the innocence of youth and the optimism of girlhood, they truly believed it was a vow they could keep. In the distance, thunder rumbled, sounding like Fate's laughter as dark clouds moved to steal the moonlight from the sky.

Chapter One

The pains began the moment her plane touched down at the Cheyenne, Wyoming, airport. By the time she got into the back of the cab to carry her to the Connor ranch, the pains shot through her with a regularity that terrified her.

"Lady, are you okay?" The driver frowned at her in his rearview mirror. "You ain't gonna have that baby right here in my cab, are you?"

"I certainly hope not." She rubbed her protruding stomach and drew in a deep breath. "How much farther to the Connor ranch?"

"Not far, just over the next hill." As if sensing her imminent delivery, the driver stepped on the gas, encouraging the old car to go faster.

She leaned her head against the seat, willing herself to try to relax, drawing air deep into her lungs. The pain battled with fear, the fear that had ridden her like a demon since that morning she'd awakened in a hotel room in Las Vegas.

Shivering, she remembered that moment when sleep had fallen away and she'd sat up in the bed, not knowing where she was or how she had gotten there.

More frightening was the realization that she had no idea who she was, only that she was very pregnant and had no memory of anything beyond that moment in time.

A purse lying on the end of the bed had held the answer to who she was. The driver's license inside had displayed a photo of her with the name of Colette Connor. Unfortunately, the license hadn't answered many other questions, like how she had come to be in the hotel room and whose baby she carried.

A suitcase had yielded clothes, an envelope of money and letters written to her and mailed from a ranch in Wyoming. The ranch was the same address as the one on her driver's license. Not knowing what else to do, Colette had hopped a plane to Cheyenne, hoping she would find welcome and answers at the Connor ranch.

As the driver turned off onto a dirt road, Colette grabbed her stomach and swallowed a moan as another pain ripped through her. Tears blurred her vision as she rode the wave of pain, vaguely aware of the taxi driver's frantic muttered curse from the front seat.

"Hang tight, missy," the driver exclaimed, pulling her back to the present. "The Connor ranch is just ahead."

Colette sat up straighter, hoping the landscape would jog her errant memory. A flat plain of scrub grass stretched out seemingly endless. The only break in the monotony was buttes of rock jutting upward and the distant foothills of a mountain range.

Nothing. No sudden flash of insight, no burst of released memories. Nothing. Dammit, what had happened to her to steal her memories? Why couldn't she tear aside the black curtain that obscured her own identity?

The driver turned onto another dirt road, then crested a hill. "There it is," he said, pointing to the ranch spread out in the valley just at the foot of the hills.

Was this home? Colette wondered, fighting against another contraction, this one stealing her breath away. Would she find family here? Somebody who could fill in all the blank spaces in her mind? Would she find a man waiting for her, frantic with worry? She wore no wedding or engagement ring but that didn't mean there wasn't a special someone in her life. So where was he now? Why was she alone?

They crossed beneath a wooden sign announcing Welcome and the driver passed a number of outbuildings and corrals before pulling to a stop in front of a sprawling ranch house.

The driver, obviously eager to be rid of her, hurried from his seat and unloaded her suitcase from the trunk. Colette didn't move. Despite the viselike contraction that squeezed her, the physical pain couldn't touch the fear that riveted through her as she stared at the unfamiliar house. What if she wasn't welcome here? Maybe her family had disowned her, thrown her from the house months before. What if there was nobody here who would help her?

She jumped as a tall blond woman walked out of the house, a smile of welcome on her lips as she approached the taxi. Colette's heart beat rapidly as an odd familiarity whispered through her. She opened the door and with an effort stepped out. Leaning against the cab, she wrapped her arms around her burgeoning stomach as another pain stabbed through her.

The smile of welcome fell from the woman's lips, replaced by shocked recognition. "Colette? Oh, my God." She raced to Colette's side and placed an arm around her. With a single glance she assessed the situation. "Cody," she yelled to the little boy lingering on the porch, "run and get Doctor Washburn. Tell him Aunt Colette is home and it appears she's about to deliver a baby." Without hesitation he took off running toward one of the outbuildings.

"Please…help me," Colette whispered weakly.

"Shh, of course we're going to help you." The woman's arms offered additional feelings of familiarity, and Colette knew whoever she was, she was somebody important in Colette's life. "Bulldog," the woman yelled. A tall, thickset young man rounded the side of the house, his moon-shaped face unlined save a vacant smile.

"Abby, can I help?" The deep masculine voice came from one side of Colette. She turned her head to see a tall, raven-haired cowboy. A faint coating of dust and dark stubble covered well-defined features. Somehow Colette knew with a certainty that beneath his five o'clock shadow hid a dimple in his chin. A black wide-brimmed hat obscured his eyes, but as he reached out a hand and touched the swell of her belly, she hissed inwardly.

Her breath caught in her throat and for just a moment she felt as though she'd run right into the arms of danger—she hadn't escaped. The thought was alien, nonsensical and quickly swallowed by another crashing wave of contraction that nearly bent her double.

"I think we can handle it," Abby said to the cowboy. "Bulldog, please carry Colette up to her room. And, Bulldog…be gentle."

"Yes, ma'am, Ms. Abby." With the ease of Hercules, the round-faced man called Bulldog swept Colette up into his arms. As he carried her to the front door, she was vaguely aware of Abby paying the cabdriver and sending him on his way.

She looked over Bulldog's shoulder, seeking the cowboy who'd startled her, but he was nowhere to be found, making her wonder if he'd been a figment of her pain-crazed mind.

The names—Abby, Cody, Bulldog—all rang distant chords of memory, and Colette felt if she could just have a moment without the pains she could pull it all together, remember everything. But the pain was constant, feeling as if it would rip her apart, tear her asunder.

As Bulldog gently placed her on the bed in a small bedroom, she felt all rational thought dissipate beneath the overriding torment of giving birth.

Her body was beyond her control, as was her mind, and she gave herself up to the primal instinct of survival.

It didn't take her long to lose track of time. The pains came one after another and despite the fact that Dr. Washburn kept assuring her she was doing fine, she feared she would die. The thought of dying without knowing who she was, who the baby's father was, why she couldn't remember, caused her to hold tight to Abby's hand. Through her moans, she tried to tell

Abby about her confusion, but knew she wasn't making sense.

"Push, Colette," Abby coached. "Come on, you can do it. Push."

The words echoed in Colette's mind. Instantly a splintered memory filled her head....

"Push, Colette. Come on, Belinda and I can't do it all alone." The wagon was heavy, laden with treasures and goodies for a picnic beneath the dragon tree. Belinda and Abby were pulling and Colette was at the rear to push the wagon up the hill. But whenever her sisters weren't looking, Colette sat on the edge of the wagon, getting a brief ride until one of them turned around and yelled at her once again.

"I CAN SEE the head. Come on, honey. Just a little bit more," Abby encouraged, and as she had so many years before, Colette did what her big sister bid. She drew in a deep breath, then bore down, screaming in relief as Abby shouted triumphantly and the baby cried a lusty hello to the world.

"It's a girl," Abby exclaimed, tears glistening in her eyes as she wiped Colette's forehead with a damp cloth. "Oh, Colette, you did a terrific job and you've got a beautiful daughter."

The doctor placed the tiny child in a blanket that smelled of sunshine and fresh air and laid her in the crook of Colette's arms. Euphoric joy suffused Colette as she looked at the child...her daughter. A wealth of dark hair covered the little head, and solemn deep blue eyes regarded Colette in an expression something between wisdom and amusement. It was as if the child, in the moments after birth, possessed all the answers of the universe.

With a yawn the baby nestled against the warmth of Colette's body and closed her eyes. Fierce protectiveness welled up inside Colette and she stroked the tiny face with a gentle finger. This baby, this child, had no name and no memories, born to a mother who had no recollection of her own past. She stared at the little face, wondering if the baby resembled her daddy. Oh, God, where was the father? Why hadn't he been with her? Who was he? Why couldn't she remember?

Tears burned hot and she blinked them away, refusing to give in to the despair that clawed at her insides. She needed answers. More importantly, she needed to find out why she felt as if she were running from something…or someone.

DAMN HER!

Hank Cooper would have given anything to unleash the most vulgar string of curse words his twisted mind could create, but instead he sank onto a bench outside the barn. The late afternoon sun washed his back and shoulders with a balmy warmth. He half smiled sardonically, too bad the warmth would never penetrate into his soul. He'd thought she might come back here, back to her roots, back to the ranch. He was rarely wrong.

He swept his hat off his head and slapped it against his knee, his thoughts whirling like dust across the prairie. He didn't think she'd recognized him, but he knew better than to trust her. Still, he'd seen no recognition in her eyes, not even when he'd touched her.

He clenched his hand, trying not to think of that moment when his hand had gently touched her stomach.

He'd been shocked when he'd seen her get out of the taxi, her stomach protruded, her features twisted in pain. Although he'd known she was pregnant, the reality of her physical condition hadn't hit him until he'd seen her ready to give birth.

"Hi, Hank."

Hank looked up to see Bulldog, his round face decorated with his usual friendly smile. Hank nodded curtly, not particularly interested in company.

Bulldog sat next to Hank, the bench creaking beneath his sturdy weight. "Want one?" he asked, holding out a handful of peppermint candy. Hank shook his head. Bulldog popped several pieces into his mouth. "Colette came home," he said, sending toward Hank the sweet scent of the candy.

"I know."

"She's been gone a long time. I missed her." The tips of Bulldog's ears reddened slightly. "I always thought she was so pretty. She had a baby." His smile transformed into a scowl. "I hope some man didn't wrong her. I'd kill anyone who hurt Colette."

And I won't let anyone get in my way, Hank thought.

"Sure you don't want one?" Bulldog offered the candy again.

"No, thanks."

"Well, I gotta get back to work." Bulldog stood and smiled. The gesture lit up his moonlike face, added depth to his rather vacant gaze. "It's gonna be nice around here with Colette back and a new baby in the house. Yes, sir, things are gonna be just fine."

With a tuneless whistle, Bulldog waved, then strode off.

Hank watched the big man until he disappeared into the barn, then he turned his attention to the house. His hands clenched at his sides as he thought of how Colette had gotten away from him, sneaking away like a thief in the night. It amazed him that she'd honestly believed she could elude him, that he would let her slink away and forget about everything. If she thought he would just let her go, she was sadly mistaken.

His gaze sought the window of her bedroom. White curtains moved in the slight breeze but no sound drifted from the interior. Colette. And now a baby. Another problem.

Consciously he took a deep breath. That was all behind him now. She was here and he wasn't about to lose track of her again.

A HAND STROKING HER, creating flames of delight as it touched her, caressed her. The hand was achingly familiar…a lover's hand and Colette knew it belonged to the man she loved, her baby's father. She struggled to open her eyes, wanting to see him, but her eyelids were too heavy. She touched his face, feeling bold features, sensual lips, the small indention in his chin.

Suddenly the hands no longer stroked, but rather imprisoned, exerting painful pressure. Fear choked her throat as she struggled to get free. "Help me," she cried.

"Come on, Colette, you can do it," Abby's voice came from far away.

"Please help me," Colette screamed. *The pressure disappeared and she sobbed in relief. As she brought her hands up to her face, she saw the blood. Her hands were covered with blood.*

With a gasp, Colette woke up. The golden light of dusk painted the room and the baby was snuggled in her arms.

"A dream," she murmured, trying to dismiss the disturbing sleep visions. Still, the fear surged upward, leaving a foul taste in her mouth as she wondered where she'd been, what she'd done. According to her license, she was twenty-two years old. Her life consisted of nothing more than a name, an age and an abiding fear.

She started as the door to the bedroom cracked open, then relaxed as Abby stuck her head in. "Oh, good. You're awake. How do you feel?"

"Tired mixed with a million other emotions," Colette admitted.

Abby walked across the room and sat in the chair at the side of the bed. "Okay, baby sister. Want to tell me where the hell you've been for the last ten months?" She reached out and took Colette's hand in hers, her dark blue eyes solemn. "I've been worried sick about you since you quit writing to me."

Although Colette sensed she could trust this woman with her very life, she found it difficult to confess the depths of her mental confusion. What if she told Abby she had amnesia and Abby tried to take the baby from her? What if it wasn't really amnesia but some sort of mental illness? And yet, what choice did she have but to tell? With all the blank spots in her mind, there was no way she could pretend everything was all right.

Within minutes she'd told Abby everything she knew, which wasn't much. Abby asked questions, her hand still holding tight to Colette's, giving unspoken emotional support and letting Colette know she'd made the right choice in coming here. "I'll have Doc Washburn give you a full examination, see if there's any physical reason for your amnesia," Abby said when Colette had finished explaining everything. "In the meantime, I'll send for Belinda."

"Belinda?"

"Our sister." She smiled sympathetically at Colette's frustration. "She'll be here soon, then we can all powwow under the dragon tree."

"The dragon tree." Colette looked at Abby. "I remember that…we had a picnic one time beneath the tree."

Abby smiled and in her eyes Colette saw pleasant memories and wished she had them, as well. "Every important occasion in our lives was talked about and shared beneath that tree." She scribbled something on a piece of paper, folded it and stuck it in an envelope. "I'll send this off tomorrow and by the end of the week Belinda should be here."

"Where is she now?"

"About a year before you decided you wanted to go to California, Belinda decided to try her hand at living on her own in Kansas City. I spoke to her last week and she was between jobs and sounded homesick. I think she'll welcome a reason to come home."

"And I was living in California?"

Abby nodded. "You moved there about a year and

a half ago. You got a job as a paralegal with a big law firm. Until about ten months ago, you wrote regularly, sounded happy and secure. Then your letters stopped coming and your phone was disconnected. My letters started coming back unopened, stamped 'addressee unknown.' I've been frantic with worry, but didn't know how to find you. Every day I prayed you'd show up safe and sound.''

Again a whisper of fear danced up Colette's spine. Why had she stopped writing? Why had her phone been disconnected? And what had she been doing in a motel room in Las Vegas? Dammit, why couldn't she remember? What had happened to steal her memories from her? She looked down at the baby sleeping at her side, the fear no longer a whisper but a shout. ''Abby, I think I'm in trouble.''

''What makes you think that?'' Once again Abby sat and reached for her hand.

''I—I don't know. It's just a feeling I have.'' More than a feeling, it was a certain knowledge in her head. ''I'm so scared.''

''That's only natural.'' Abby offered her a smile of reassurance. ''Honey, you're suffering a memory loss and that has to be frightening. You're safe here, and I'm sure it's just a matter of time before your memory comes back.''

''Abby, do you know who is the father of my baby? Am I married?''

Abby squeezed her hand. ''I don't know,'' she answered softly. ''I don't know what happened to you in the months we lost contact.'' She smiled, but the gesture looked forced. ''It will all be okay, Colette.''

She released Colette's hand and stood. "Now, I'll get out of here and let you get some more sleep."

Colette nodded although she didn't believe Abby's words. Nothing was going to be okay. Her fear came from more than her lack of memory, it came from her gut, a visceral terror she couldn't ignore. When Abby had left the room, Colette snuggled the baby closer to her side, knowing with the instincts of prey that someplace was a hunter, looking for her and her baby.

As THE SUN SET, it lengthened shadows and formed pockets of darkness on the east side of the bunkhouse. A lone figure leaned against the planked wooden building, his gaze focused on the bedroom window where white lace curtains billowed inward with the night breeze.

He'd known she'd show up here sooner or later. It was the obvious place for her to come. She was smart, she was crafty, but she'd made a big mistake in being predictable and coming home.

He scuffed his snakeskin boot against the ground, impatience gnawing inside him, absently tracing the calluses he'd developed in the time he'd been working at the ranch.

It had been luck that had gotten him hired here a month ago. However, he wouldn't depend on luck any longer. He had a job to do, and he couldn't afford to screw up. Too much was at risk. She wouldn't escape from him again.

Chapter Two

"How come it had to be a girl?" Cody, Abby's six-year-old son, stood by the side of the crib. He sighed and turned to look at Colette. "There's already too many dumb girls in this house. My Mom, and Maria and Aunt Belinda and you…" He thrust a thumb back at the crib. "And now this new one." He shook his head ruefully. "Too many girls."

Colette bit her tongue to suppress a smile, knowing Cody took this girl thing very seriously. In the ten days she'd been at the ranch, he still hadn't quite forgiven her for giving birth to a girl instead of a boy.

She checked to make sure the baby was still sleeping, then walked with Cody out into the hallway. "You know, Cody, someday baby Brook might need a big strong cousin to protect her."

Cody frowned thoughtfully, then scuffed the toe of his worn cowboy boot against the floor. "Brook is my onliest cousin, isn't she?"

"Yes, she is."

Cody's blue eyes sparked and his chest puffed with pride. "I'm a cowboy, and cowboys always protect their cousins."

Colette smiled. "That's great, Cody. I feel much better knowing Brook can always depend on you." She patted his back. "Now, why don't you run on downstairs and see what Maria has made for breakfast this morning? I'll be down in just a few minutes."

"Okay. I'll see you later, Aunt Colette." He raced down the hallway, his boots clattering on the wooden floors. Colette watched until he disappeared around the corner, then went into her bedroom to check on Brook one last time before joining the others for breakfast.

She went to the crib, still awed by the fact that the child sleeping within was hers. Brook Ann Connor. She didn't know where the name Brook had come from, only that it was the name she wanted for her daughter.

Brook was a good baby. It was as if she knew the tenuous hold her mother had on sanity and so compensated by being a contented, happy baby who slept long hours and rarely fussed at all.

Although no real memories had resurfaced over the past ten days, Colette had found a measure of peace simply being among people who obviously loved her.

Belinda had arrived four days before, and since her arrival the three sisters had spent hours talking. For Colette it was a study in frustration, to hear things from her past—names and events—and feel nothing. She cried when Abby and Belinda spoke of their parents' funeral, mourning a mother and father not remembered and long dead.

Leaning down, she kissed Brook on the cheek, picked up the portable monitor, then left the room and headed for the large dining room at the other end of the house.

"Good morning," she greeted Belinda, who was already seated at the large oak table with a cup of coffee in hand. Cody sat next to her, focused on his plateful of pancakes. "Where's Abby?" she asked, pouring herself a cup of coffee from the pot that sat on a warmer on the sideboard.

"She's going over last-minute details with our foreman, Rusty. We've got a group coming in from Phoenix for a week. They're supposed to arrive sometime this afternoon." Belinda paused to take a sip of her coffee, then continued, "But she told me to tell you she hasn't forgotten her offer to watch Brook for a couple of hours this morning so you can get out and see the ranch. She thinks maybe that will help jog something loose in your memory. Besides, you've been cooped up inside for too long. Fresh air and sunshine will be good for you."

"Dr. Washburn feels that eventually something will jog my memory," Colette exclaimed. "I just hope that something happens soon." She sank into the chair across from Belinda. "There's nothing worse than having big black holes in your mind."

"I hate to have holes in my socks," Cody quipped, causing both his aunts to laugh.

"At least we know it's nothing physical," Belinda said.

Colette nodded, then smiled a good morning to Maria, the cook, who entered the room with a plate of pancakes for Colette and Belinda. Cody kept up a steady stream of chatter, excited at the prospect of new guests and hoping there would be a boy his age. He finished eating and left the table in minutes.

"I wonder if we ate that fast when we were that age," Belinda said as she poured syrup over her pancakes.

"Who knows?" Colette sipped her coffee, thoughtfully staring at her sister. "Belinda, I feel silly asking you this, but you don't know who I was dating…who might be Brook's father, do you?"

"No, I don't. You weren't involved with anyone before you left here, so it had to be somebody you met while in California."

Colette sighed. She'd hoped Belinda would have answers, but she knew it had been a long shot. "What about you? Are you married…dating…in love?"

Belinda laughed. "None of the above." Her smile faltered slightly. "Although I was once in love, but that was a long time ago and he doesn't even live in the area any longer."

"I'm sure I was in love with Brook's father," Colette said firmly. Any other scenario was unthinkable.

"Don't worry, Colette. Dr. Washburn said your amnesia was probably caused by stress or some sort of emotional trauma. Now that you're back here at the ranch, safe and sound, it will all come back to you."

Colette nodded and stared down at her plate. Yes, that's what Dr. Washburn had said, and that's what scared her. Even being back at the ranch with the security of home and family, she was afraid. Somehow she knew she was far from being safe.

THE SUN WARMED Colette's face and the air smelled like cattle and horses, fresh hay and sweet grass.

Again she found it difficult to believe she'd chosen to leave the ranch and all its beauty behind for a job in California.

As she walked by the barn, a man stepped out of the dark interior. As the sun hit his face fully, it highlighted bold, almost savage features: a straight nose and high cheekbones and a mouth that looked as if it had never formed a smile. His face was weathered by the sun and chiseled by hard knocks. Unlike many of the working men, he wore no hat and his ebony hair nearly touched his shoulders. His gaze met Colette's.

Instantly fear formed in the pit of her stomach and rocketed throughout her body. Those eyes. She knew those dark eyes. She suddenly remembered he was the same man she'd seen in those first moments of arriving at the ranch.

With Brook's birth she'd forgotten all about that moment of inexplicable fear. Now fear rocked through her. *Danger! Danger!* The word screamed in her head.

The man held her gaze with frightening intensity. Suddenly another emotion shimmied up her spine, weakening her knees. Passion, as strong, as intense as the fear. She knew him…somehow, someway, she knew this man. But how? From where?

Her foot caught in a rut and she felt herself pitch forward. Colette hit the graveled path on her hands and knees.

"Hey, there, are you all right?" An unfamiliar voice and a strong hand helped her up.

Colette smiled in embarrassment at the pleasant-faced man who helped her regain her feet. His cowboy hat hid his hair, but his blond mustache gleamed in the sunshine and his mouth curved upward in a pleasing smile. "Thanks. I can't believe I'm such a klutz," she said, brushing the gravel off her jeans.

"No problem. I'm Roger Eaton." He held out his hand. "I was hired a couple weeks ago to be in charge of the horseback riding for the guests."

Colette nodded absently, her gaze seeking the man who had caused her to trip and fall. He'd disappeared, leaving behind only a residual boom of anxiety still resounding in Colette's chest.

"Come on, we'd better get you inside," Roger said. "You've scraped your palms and they need to be cleaned up."

Colette looked at the palms of her hands, realizing he was right. Blood oozed from several places where the gravel had broken the skin. She looked away, the sight of the blood making her ill. She thanked Roger for his help, then hurried toward the house.

Belinda greeted her, dismayed as she saw Colette's hands. "I'll clean you up," Belinda said as she led Colette into one of the bathrooms. "You've never been very good about dealing with blood."

"I think I just figured that out," Colette agreed. She turned her head, wincing as Belinda cleaned her palms with antiseptic.

As Belinda worked, Colette replayed in her mind the moment of seeing the dark cowboy. What was it about him that had caused terror to eddy through her? Terror and a strange singing passion? Like the memory of an old song, it was as if she could remember the tune, but was unable to remember the words. Was it possible she knew him? Was he part of the past she couldn't remember? What part did he play in her life? Had she dated him, been intimate with him? Or did he just remind her of somebody else?

Confusion muddied her mind, but one thing remained clear. If she knew the man, if he was part of her obscured past, she couldn't dismiss the potent terror she'd felt when she'd seen him.

Something about him had frightened her and she had the distinct impression of danger whispering against the nape of her neck.

She had to remember. Whoever he was, he scared her and there had to be a reason for that. She had to get her memories back. She had a feeling her life just might depend on it.

HANK POURED more oil on the saddle on the wooden workhorse. With a soft rag he swirled the oil across the worn leather.

"Don't you ever rest?"

Hank looked up as Roger Eaton entered the barn. "I like to keep busy," he answered, focusing on his task.

Roger leaned against the door and shook out a cigarette.

"Don't light that in here." Hank looked at him in irritation. Any fool who'd spent more than ten minutes working on a ranch would know better than to light a cigarette in a barn full of hay.

"Sorry, wasn't thinking." He tucked the pack of cigarettes back into his pocket. "I met the elusive Colette today. Heard she has amnesia. Heard she doesn't remember anything at all before the day she arrived here."

"Sounds to me like you've been listening to gossip." Hank poured more oil on the leather.

"Yeah, well I'll tell you something that's not gossip. She's a hell of a looker. I'll bet she could make a man forget his name, if you know what I mean."

Hank rubbed the saddle harder.

"Yes, sir, a sexy lady like that could make me forget my name and address." Roger kicked at a pile of straw. "Wonder what happened to her that put her in such a state? Like something just scared the memories right out of her. Weird, right?"

Hank grunted, irritated to realize he'd been rubbing the same place for the duration of the conversation. He looked at Roger. "Is there a particular reason for this conversation or did you just want to waste my time?"

Roger's eyes widened, then narrowed. "You're an unfriendly bastard, Cooper."

"That's what they tell me," Hank agreed.

"Think I'll go have my smoke and find some better company." Without a backward glance, Roger left the barn. Hank felt no remorse. He wasn't here to make friends.

Amnesia. He thought of that moment when he'd first stepped out of the barn and his gaze had caught hers. Had he seen the flicker of recognition in her eyes? He wasn't sure.

He wondered if she really had amnesia or was only faking. It would be just like her to fake it, pretend not to remember anything, then run when she got the chance.

In any case, if she did run again, he would find her. No matter where she tried to hide.

"ABBY? Can I talk to you for a minute?" Colette peeked into the office, where Abby sat at a desk, an account book opened in front of her.

"Sure, I could use a break." She closed the account book and stood. "In fact, why don't we go to the kitchen and see if there's any of that cherry cobbler left, something to take the bad taste of ranch finances out of my mouth."

The kitchen had quickly become Colette's favorite room in the house. Large and airy, with a huge oak table, the ambience was warm and inviting. As Abby raided the refrigerator, Colette poured them each a cup of coffee, then together they sat at the table.

"Whew, what a day," Abby said, wrapping her hands around the coffee mug and leaning back in her chair.

"I saw all the guests arriving. Did they get settled in okay?"

Abby nodded. "I think it's going to be a fun group. They're all family, here for a reunion. At least with them, I can put off letting some of the workers go for a few more weeks."

"Things are that bad?" Colette asked.

Abby nodded. "Short of pulling magic money out of a hat, I'm not sure how we'll make it through the next year."

"I told Belinda this afternoon that I was going to talk to you about taking over the baby-sitting for the guests. I noticed there were a couple of small children in the group that arrived. It's the least I can do to help."

"That would be terrific," Abby agreed. "I'd twisted Belinda's arm to take care of the baby-sitting, but I want to use her marketing savvy and put her to work on a brochure for advertising.'' She paused a moment to dip them each a generous helping of the cherry cobbler. ''We've got a playroom set up in the community building. It has everything you should need.''

For the next few minutes Abby conveyed how the service worked, explaining that the guests signed up for baby-sitting needs on a sheet posted at the community building.

''Brook asleep?'' Abby asked.

Colette smiled and nodded. ''She's such a good baby.'' As always, thoughts of Brook brought a wealth of frustration, as well. ''I just wish…it's so disturbing not to know who her father is, what he meant to me and where he is now.''

Abby frowned and rubbed her forehead tiredly. ''Maybe there are things best left not remembered. There are times I wish I remembered nothing about Cody's father.''

''What happened to him?'' Colette asked, hoping the question wasn't out of line.

''Greg rode off into the sunset when Cody was just a few weeks old,'' Abby explained, her voice holding a trace of bitterness. ''He didn't see himself as the father type. So, we divorced, I took back my maiden name, and I've raised Cody alone.''

Colette reached across the table and touched Abby's shoulder. ''I'm sorry.''

Abby shrugged and took a deep breath, her shoulders stiffening as if she summoned some measurement of inner strength. ''Most of the time it's not too bad. I adore Cody and wouldn't change his presence in my life for the world. Just occasionally a memory comes back to haunt me, makes me think of how things could have been had Greg been a different kind of man.'' She shrugged again, then drained her coffee cup. ''Well, I'd better get back to work. I've got another hour or two of work ahead of me before I can call it a night.''

She started to carry the dishes from the table to the sink, but Colette stopped her. ''I'll do that. You go on and get your work finished.''

''Thanks.'' Abby flashed her a quicksilver smile and started out of the kitchen.

''Abby? Could I ask you for a favor?''

She turned back and looked at Colette. ''Sure. What?''

''Could you give me a list of all the people who work here at the ranch?''

Abby's forehead wrinkled with curiosity. ''Sure, but why?''

''I'd just like to learn everyone's names,'' she hedged, reluctant to admit that she thought she'd recognized one of the cowboys in case she'd been mistaken. ''Without any of my memories I feel like my head is empty. I guess I figure I can fill it up with the people who are in my present.''

Abby nodded. ''Stop by the office on your way to bed. I'll have a list for you.''

It took Colette only a few minutes to clean up the dishes. As she worked, she thought of the dark-haired cowboy with the haunting shadowy eyes. Of course, there was no way by looking at a list of names she'd know immediately which name was his. She hoped by looking at the names, one would jump out and ring a bell of recognition.

However, she was also aware of the fact that she might have been mistaken in thinking she knew the cowboy. He might simply bare a passing resemblance to somebody in her past.

Later that night she sat in her room, the light on the desk illuminating the list of names Abby had provided to her. There was a total of seventeen names. Three female, the rest males.

Abby had marked the names of the men she'd hired in the last month. There were five. Roger Eaton, Bob Sanderson, Philip Weiss, Hank Cooper and Billy Sims. The names meant nothing to her, although she wondered vaguely which name went with the dark cowboy. She'd met Roger, who'd helped her up when she'd fallen, but he's the only name she could attach with a face.

She sighed in frustration, realizing no matter how long, how hard she stared at the list, nothing changed. Stretching with arms overhead, she stood and walked over to the crib. As always, her heart expanded as she gazed at her sleeping daughter.

Brook slept on her tummy, a thumb stuck in her mouth. Her sweet baby scent wafted on the air, filling Colette's sense with the headiness of a love so pure, so clean, it ached inside her. She stroked the dark down that covered Brook's head. "Sweet baby," she whispered.

She fought the impulse to pick her up, snuggle Brook against her heart. Did it really matter that she couldn't remember her past? She could be as strong as Abby, raise Brook as a single parent. Surely if

Brook's father was a loving, caring man, he'd be here. She wouldn't have been alone in a Las Vegas hotel room. If he'd loved Colette, wanted the baby, he would have shown up by now.

Sighing heavily, she turned from the crib and went into the adjoining bathroom. As she washed her face, she stared at her reflection, trying to find a resemblance to Abby and Belinda. Both her sisters had blond hair, while Colette's was a chestnut brown. Their eyes were blue and hers were hazel.

Still, she thought she saw a likeness in the shape of her face, a sameness in the contour of her lips. It comforted her. Without her memories she felt displaced, groundless, but her familial ties to Belinda and Abby soothed her, gave her emotional sustenance.

She changed from her clothes into a long, white cotton nightgown, then went into the bedroom. The near full moon beckoned, spilling silvery light through the window. She pulled the curtains aside and gazed out. The landscape looked surreal in the light.

The clicking of insects, the hushed whisper of a night breeze and the distant lowing of the cattle drifted in through the open window. Comforting night noises. She wrapped her arms around herself and leaned against the window frame, her gaze still directed out the window.

Feeling more at peace than she had since her arrival, she started to turn away from the window, but paused as a flicker of movement captured her gaze.

There, by the edge of the barn. She squinted, trying to pierce the dark shadows of night. Yes, she was certain. There was somebody standing there, staring toward her window. She could almost feel the intensity of his gaze prickling on her skin.

As she watched, a match flared then died, producing the red glow of a lit cigarette. Was he watching her window? Or merely leaning against the barn for a quick smoke?

Suddenly realizing that with the desk lamp lit she was probably perfectly silhouetted in the window frame, she pulled the curtains tightly closed and moved away.

She shut off the desk lamp, then crawled into bed, still disturbed. Even if the man outside wasn't staring at her window or watching her, she realized she could never be completely happy or safe without her memories.

Something in her past threatened her. She didn't know what or who. She only knew until she remembered her past, she would never know when her present happiness might be shattered.

Chapter Three

Colette leaned on the top of the main corral railing, Brook in her arms, her gaze captured by the man riding the back of a skittish horse.

A huge, powerful creature, the horse sidestepped and shook his head as if fighting whatever command the rider gave.

Despite the magnificence of the horse, it was the rider who captured Colette's attention. He appeared to be an extension of the horse, his dark hair the same color as the animal he rode. His T-shirt stretched across his broad back, and his biceps bulged as he worked the reins in an effort to control.

Even his legs appeared taut within the worn jeans that covered them, giving the appearance of unsuppressed strength.

Although she was too far away to see his eyes, she remembered them from her brief encounter with him the day before. She knew his dark eyes were framed by thick black lashes, and she couldn't deny there had been danger in their depths, a danger mingled with an indefinable emotion that had stirred a latent desire in her. What was it about him that caused such an odd mixture of emotions in her?

She'd dreamed of eyes the night before. Dark, angry eyes. They stared at her, emanating an unspoken threat that terrified her. She'd wanted to run, needed to get away—escape his anger, escape the rage in those eyes—but she couldn't move. Something held her confined. His prisoner. Fear had kept her still, fear and something else, something more powerful. Lust. Desire.

She jumped as a hand touched her shoulder. She turned to see Roger Eaton standing next to her.

"Good morning. Abby sent me out to take you to the community center," he explained with a friendly smile.

She nodded and placed Brook in the carrier on the ground next to where she stood. Picking up the carrier, she straightened, her gaze once again on the cowboy on horseback.

"Who is that man?" she asked Roger.

"Hank. Hank Cooper. Your sister hired him about a month ago. A week after she hired me. He's good with the horses. According to your sister, that particular horse hadn't ever been ridden, but Hank's been working with her since the first day he arrived." Roger laughed. "You should have seen him the first day he got on her back. She bucked him off in a matter of seconds. Hank didn't look so hot lying flat on his back in the dust."

Colette looked at Roger curiously. "You don't like him much, do you?"

Roger shrugged. "He's a hard man to like. Keeps

to himself and doesn't offer much in the way of friendship. Of course, there's several like that here.''

Colette redirected her attention to the horse and rider, wondering what it was about the man that disturbed her so much. He was handsome in a brutal sort of way, looking as strong and enduring as the mountains in the distance. But it was more than his attractiveness that troubled her. Something about him distressed her, but she couldn't put her finger on exactly what it was.

''Do you know where he's from?'' she asked.

Roger shook his head. ''We'd better get going, I've got work to do.''

She nodded and they started on their way. As they passed the barn, Colette noticed several cigarette butts lying in the dirt in about the area she'd spotted somebody standing in the darkness the night before. Again a nervous tremor raced through her. Had the man she'd seen been watching her? Had he stood here and smoked cigarette after cigarette, his eyes trained on her window? Who had it been?

Stop it, she commanded herself. She was spooking herself with thoughts that might have no basis in reality. Just because there were several cigarette butts there in the dirt didn't mean they had all been smoked by somebody staring at her window. Probably the men weren't allowed to smoke in the barn, where hay and grain were stored. She was being ridiculous, looking for a bogeyman where there was none.

''Here we are,'' Roger said as he opened the door to the community building. They entered a large, airy room and he pointed to a nearby doorway. ''The playroom is through there. Is there anything I can do for you before I leave?''

''No, I'll be fine. Thanks for showing me the way.''

''No problem.'' He tipped his hat, then turned and walked away.

Colette watched him go. He seemed like a nice young man. She wondered how long he'd stick around. Abby had complained only the night before about how difficult it was to keep good ranch help. Would Roger last through the fall? Or would he be one of the ones Abby had to let go because of finances? It seemed a catch-22 for Abby. She couldn't afford to pay terrific wages to keep good help, and so went through a huge turnover of workers.

Just before he disappeared from her sight, he paused. As she watched, he shook out a cigarette from his pocket and lit it. Again Colette felt a shiver work up her spine. Had it been Roger she'd seen the night before? Had it been he who'd stood there in the darkness, watching her at her window?

One more time Colette felt the breath of danger caress the back of her neck. She had to get her memory back. She had to know if she and Brook were safe or if somebody was out to get them.

HANK MOVED the brush down the powerful horse's flank, uttering soothing murmurs as he worked. He'd been amazed by how easily his horse skills had returned to him. Like riding a bicycle, it had only taken mounting a horse again to remember all the things his mother had taught him.

Putting the young mare in her stable, his thoughts

turned to Colette. He'd seen her pass the corral early in the morning with Roger Eaton, their destination apparently the community building.

He had to figure out what he was going to do about her, had to decide his next course of action. If the amnesia was true, then she wasn't as much of a risk. If she didn't remember him, then she probably wouldn't run again. But there was no way to know for certain. And that left him uncertain as to how to proceed.

He needed to force a confrontation with her; see if she remembered him or not. He wanted to meet her face to face, examine her reaction, peer into her eyes.

Putting a cupful of oats in the feed trough, he then left the barn. He walked toward the community center, unsure exactly what he had in mind, but following instincts long honed.

He'd always worked on instinct, found gut reaction far more reliable than anything else. It was part of what made him so good at what he did, part of what kept him alive.

The door to the community building stood open and he walked inside, his gaze focused on the playroom. He heard no sounds, nothing to indicate she was still here. But when he entered the playroom the first thing he saw was the baby in the crib.

She was awake, lying on her back, making little soft sounds of sweetness. He approached the crib, his heart suddenly pounding loud in his ears.

Clad in a pink one-piece sleeper, the little girl eyed him solemnly. He could smell her, a mixture of baby powder and innocence that pierced through the armor around his heart. She had dark eyes that matched the dark hair on her head.

He hadn't expected the visceral pull, the utter wonder that swirled inside him as he stared at the baby girl. Such a tiny thing, with perfect, miniature features.

Leaning down, he lightly touched her cheek, a smile curving his lips as she turned her head and worked her mouth as if seeking a bottle. "Hey, little one," he said softly, irritated that he didn't even know her name. Damn Colette. There was no getting around it. The baby was a definite complication. Another stake in a game with no rules.

Gently, he picked her up, wanting to hold her close for just a moment, feel her wiggly warmth against his heart. He had no idea what the future held for Colette or this innocent child.

He closed his eyes and breathed in the scent of her, imprinting it in his brain. Her little bottom fit perfectly in the palm of his hand and she snuggled against his chest in complete trust.

She didn't know she'd been born in the midst of chaos, couldn't know her life was at risk. She only knew the needs of a newborn and trusted those needs would be attended.

Reluctantly he placed her in the crib, smiling as her fist closed around his finger.

"What are you doing in here?" Colette's voice rang sharply from behind him.

He straightened and turned to see her standing in the doorway, Cody and two other children at her side. "I came to get some things from the closet and saw the baby and nobody else around."

"We were just outside," she replied, and moved past him to check on the baby. "Cody, why don't you and Amy and Grant get out some of the puzzles on the shelf in the closet," she suggested, then looked at Hank. She waited until the kids were occupied. "Please, get what you need and leave," she said, her voice slightly haughty.

He scrutinized her face, looking for signs of recognition. How could she not remember him? "She's a pretty little girl. Do you think she looks like you, or more like her daddy?" he asked, knowing he was baiting but unable to help himself.

Her face flushed pink. "She looks like herself. She looks like Brook."

His heart seemed to stop for a moment in his chest. "That's her name? Brook?" He moved closer to her. Damn her for working his emotions like they'd never been worked before.

He studied Colette's face, noting the high color that pinkened her cheeks. Her blue blouse gave her hazel eyes a tinge of blueness and emphasized a new fullness to her breasts. If he touched her, would she remember?

As he took another step toward her, her brow furrowed in confusion and she stepped backward, as if trying to distance herself from him. Hank realized at that moment her amnesia was real, and he wondered what this development would have on the future and his job. "I'll just let you get to work," he said. Turning on his heels, he strode toward the door.

"Mr. Cooper?" Her voice made him pause and he turned to look at her. "Have...have we met before?"

Hank quickly assessed his options, knowing if he

told her yes, she'd want to know the details. It was better she not know. Not remembering those details just might save her life.

He looked at the baby in the crib. "No," he answered, then, balling his hands into fists, he turned and left.

Colette watched him go, the whisper of fear dancing inside her. Who was Hank Cooper and why did he affect her so strongly? She had the distinct feeling he'd lied, that she did know him from someplace other than this ranch.

When he'd stepped close to her she'd smelled his scent. Masculine yet with a spicy cologne that she knew she'd smelled before. Why would he lie about knowing her? What had he been in her past? And why was he so interested in Brook?

She sank onto a chair next to the crib, her attention torn between her daughter and the three children playing with puzzles on the floor. He'd said he'd come to get something out of the closet, but he hadn't taken anything with him. Why had he come here? What had he wanted?

On impulse, she picked up Brook, needing to hold her close, assure herself of the baby's safety. Mixed with the scent of baby powder and milk was the faint lingering odor of Hank Cooper's cologne.

She stood and walked with Brook to the window. Staring out, she recalled the nightmare that had plagued her the night before. The eyes she'd dreamed of...the angry eyes.

HE STOOD at the pay phone on the side of the bunkhouse, impatiently tapping a finger on the receiver as he waited for his call to be answered. He stopped the tapping as a familiar gruff voice bellowed a greeting.

"It's me," he said. "I've got news."

"It's about time," the deep voice growled.

"She's here and she has some sort of memory loss."

"I don't give a damn if she has chicken pox. She's smart, too damn smart for her own good, and she has the ability to fry me."

"What do you want me to do?" he asked, although he could have guessed the answer.

"I want her disposed of...permanently." There was a tense pause. "Hell, man, use your head. A ranch can be a dangerous place. Make it look like an accident. We don't need any other problems."

"Okay. I'll call you when it's been accomplished." He hung up the phone, then lit a cigarette. Squinting his eyes against a cloud of smoke, he contemplated what kind of an accident would befall Colette Connor.

Chapter Four

"Come on, you have to go tomorrow night. It will be good for you to get out among adults," Abby exclaimed as she poured herself another cup of coffee. "We always plan a hayride and an old-fashioned cookout on Friday nights when we have guests." She rejoined Colette at the table. "And I've already spoken to Maria about staying here with Cody and Brook."

Colette smiled, as always feeling like a willow in a windstorm around her strong, older sister. "Since you've taken care of everything, I guess I'll go on the hayride," she agreed.

"Oh, honey, you don't have to go if you don't want to." Abby frowned worriedly. "Sometimes I'm too pushy for my own good. You have to tell me to back off."

"Did I tell you to back off often in the past?" Colette asked with a grin.

"About once a day," Abby admitted with a laugh. "When you were ten you called me bossy, when you were twelve I graduated to domineering and by the time you were fifteen I'd reached the pinnacle of big sisterhood and become tyrannical.''

Colette laughed, as always an ache of wistfulness reminding her of her lack of memories. How she wished she remembered those frivolous carefree days of childhood, when her biggest problem apparently was dealing with two bossy older sisters. She picked up her coffee mug and sipped thoughtfully. ''Abby, would you tell me what you know about Hank Cooper?'' she asked.

Abby's eyebrows danced upward quizzically. ''Why?''

Colette shrugged. ''Something about him bothers me…I'm not sure what it is.''

''He hasn't gotten out of line, has he? I mean, some of the men working on the ranch think we're all fair game for a quick roll in the hay.''

''No, it's nothing like that,'' Colette replied hurriedly. She frowned and drained the last of her coffee. ''I can't exactly explain…just something about him bothers me and I was wondering what you knew about him.''

''Not much,'' Abby admitted. ''I do know he's a natural with the horses. I haven't seen his kind of talent in years. He showed up here at the ranch looking for a job about a month ago.'' Abby smiled ruefully. ''I don't ask for much in the way of references, have never cared about a man's past. If they do their jobs and keep their noses clean, I'm satisfied.''

Colette nodded, realizing nothing Abby knew could help her where Hank Cooper was concerned. Somehow, some way, she was going to have to figure out for herself why he bothered her, why it was that his eyes haunted her dreams.

"You okay?" Abby asked, her forehead once again wrinkled in concern.

"I'm fine," Colette assured her, knowing Abby had enough on her mind in running the ranch without Colette adding to her burden. They both jumped as a knock fell on the back door.

Abby got up to answer it. "Junior," she exclaimed in delight. "You've been neglecting us lately. Come in and have a cup of coffee."

The man who entered hardly looked like a "junior." Tall and barrel-shaped, he sported a head of bushy gray hair and matching eyebrows. His face was deeply tanned, and crisscrossed with wrinkles that spoke of age and life experiences.

"Hi, darlin'." He leaned over and kissed Colette on the forehead. "Heard you were back in town. Good to have you back where you belong." He thanked Abby as she set a cup of coffee in front of him, then he started talking to Abby about the ranch.

Colette listened absently, instantly drawn to the warmth of the older man's smile, but more drawn to the safety his sheriff's uniform implied. Maybe he can help, she thought. Help with what? What could she say to him? That she was in danger but didn't know why? That she was afraid somebody was after her but didn't know who?

She looked at her watch and realized she needed to go. "Excuse me, but I need to get going. I'm sitting with the kids for a couple of hours so the adults can go trail riding again."

"We'll get a chance to visit and catch up later,"

Junior said, flashing her another warm, parental kind of smile.

Minutes later Colette left the house, Brook napping in her carrier. As Colette walked toward the community building, she thought over the past couple of days. It was comforting how seamlessly she'd fit back into the routine of the ranch. She spent the days baby-sitting and caring for Brook. In the evenings the whole family ate dinner together, discussing and sharing all the aspects of their day.

Although Colette usually had little to add to the conversation, she enjoyed the camaraderie between herself and her sisters, the bond that, despite her memory lapse, had not been lost.

Only some things always managed to darken her contentment. A feeling of impending doom increased daily along with the awareness of eyes watching her every movement. That, and Hank Cooper troubled her.

As if summoned by her thoughts, Hank appeared at the side of the barn. Had he somehow known she'd be approaching at that very moment and had timed his appearance to coincide with hers?

''Good morning,'' he said as he fell into step with her.

'''Morning.'' She didn't look at him. She was torn between the strange need to somehow distance herself from him and the desire to crawl into his head to see if any of her memories resided with him. It was crazy, but somehow she had the feeling that he was a part of her forgotten past, an integral piece to a frightening puzzle.

''Would you like me to carry that for you?'' He

gestured to the diaper bag slung over the crook of her arm.

"No, thanks, I can manage. Besides, I'm sure you have other, more important chores to attend to."

He grinned, a sexy, lazy smile that caused a coil of heat to unfurl in the pit of her stomach. "I'm on a break. For the next thirty minutes my time is my own."

"What do you do in your spare time, Mr. Cooper?" she asked. *Do you stand in the darkness and watch me? Is it your gaze I feel on me? Constantly watching?*

"Please, call me Hank, and I don't have much spare time. There's always something that needs to be done on a spread this size." For a moment his gaze held hers, intense and probing, it made her feel as if he attempted to violate her mind.

With an effort, she broke away from the gaze, wondering again why she felt such an uneasy familiarity with the man. "Abby tells me she hired you about a month ago. Where's home for you?" she asked.

"Here and there. I've never had much need for a permanent home base. What about you? I heard that before you arrived here you were someplace in California."

She could still feel the heat of his gaze on her and once again her eyes met his. "If you've heard that, then you've also probably heard I have amnesia. I don't remember anything before coming here."

His smoke-dark eyes lingered a moment longer on her as a muscle jumped in his lower jaw. "Nothing?"

"Nothing." Again she averted her gaze from his as the heat in her stomach reignited and spread over her entire body. Why did he affect her this way? What was it about him that made her think of long nights of lovemaking, of tangled limbs beneath rumpled sheets?

Had he lied when he'd told her they hadn't met before? Did her unease have nothing to do with suppressed memories and everything to do with the fact that he was an enormously attractive man who oozed sex appeal?

Relief flooded her as they reached the community building and he tipped his hat in parting. She watched him go, her heart slowly resuming a more normal rhythm as he moved into the distance.

Going inside, she tried to shove thoughts of Hank Cooper out of her mind, but found him as impossible to dismiss as a case of hives. She set Brook's carrier on the table in the playroom and went to the window, unsurprised to see Hank still in viewing distance. In the past couple of days she'd noticed he always seemed near to where she was, appeared to shadow her movements whenever she left the main house.

Why? Why did Hank Cooper seem to have such interest in her? Was his attention drawn from something in the past, or merely the passing interest of a man for a woman? What man in his right mind would be interested in a woman who had no memory and had just given birth? A fleeting smile curved her lips. Who said Hank Cooper was in his right mind?

The morning passed quickly and lunchtime came and went. Late afternoon the kids left with their parents and Colette busied herself cleaning up the room.

She'd finally put everything away when the outer

door flew open and a ranch hand she'd not seen before stood in the doorway.

Thin and wiry, the man brought with him the sour smell of perspiration, stale smoke and strong alcohol as he stepped into the room. Beneath the dusty hat he wore, his brown eyes peered around the room.

"May I help you?" Colette asked, moving closer to the table where Brook rested in the carrier.

"I'm s'possed to put up shelves," he slurred, a drunken grin lifting the corners of his mouth as he eyed Colette. "You're a pretty little thing." He stumbled several steps toward her.

"I think you'd better leave and put the shelves up another time," Colette said, her voice wavering with uncertainty.

He shook his head. "Can't. Ms. Abby told me to do it today, and Ms. Abby gets plum crazy when chores don't get done." He staggered forward another couple of steps and Colette realized the man was thoroughly, completely drunk.

His grin widened as his gaze focused once again on her. "I'll bet you smell as pretty as you look." When he stepped forward again, Colette backed up, disturbed to find herself pinned between the wall and the man.

"I think you'd better go."

"Ah, come on, don't get all bossy like your sisters. Why don't you try being a little nice to me." He reached up and touched her hair. "I could be very nice to you."

His touch made her skin crawl, and the glassiness of his eyes made her aware that he might be too drunk to listen to reason. Unreasonable terror swam inside her. He was just a drunken ranch hand, but something about his unwanted closeness brought panic to the surface. "You're so pretty," he repeated, his grimy hand stroking the length of her hair, his breath rancid in her face.

She tried to sidestep him, but he grabbed her arm. "Let me go," she demanded, trying to yank her arm from his viselike grip.

"Ah, come on, don't be that way," he protested, bracing his hands on the wall on either side of her, effectively making her his prisoner.

"Sims. Let the lady go." Hank Cooper's voice rang with authority. He filled the doorway, his posture tense, his dark eyes radiating undisguised danger.

"Ah, I was just having a little fun," Sims protested.

"Well, the lady doesn't appear to be having fun." Hank stepped into the room and placed a hand on the back of the man's neck. "Get on out of here. Go back to the bunkhouse and sleep it off." Colette wasn't sure whether it was the tone of Hank's voice or the strength of his hand on Sims's neck, but Sims nodded and with Hank's assistance headed out the door.

Colette sagged against the wall, her knees trembling uncontrollably as adrenaline slowly dissipated. She shuddered as she remembered the way his body had pressed close to hers, how his arms had formed a prison to contain her. Something about the incident evoked a murmur of a memory. A memory of another time, another man pressed against her, his breath hot against her neck as he whispered threatening words into her ear.

"You okay?"

She looked to see Hank once again standing in the doorway. She nodded, afraid to move from the wall, afraid her shaking legs wouldn't hold her. "I'm fine." To her horror, tears blurred her vision and a sob shook her.

In three long strides, Hank reached her. He pulled her away from the wall and into the strength of his arms. "Billy Sims is just a drunken fool," he said. "He wouldn't have hurt you."

"I know. I don't know why I'm overreacting, but I can't help it." She leaned against Hank, finding comfort in the strong arms surrounding her, the sunshine scent of his cotton shirt and the familiarity of his spice cologne.

His embrace wasn't threatening in any way. He held her lightly, without intimacy, and yet she fought a crazy impulse to lean into him, press against the hardness of his chest. Threatened and confused by her own thoughts, she broke the embrace and stepped away from him.

"I'm so grateful you appeared when you did," she said, moving over to the table where Brook still peacefully slept. "I wasn't sure what he might have been capable of."

"I'll make sure Sims stays away from you," Hank said, the words a promise she knew he'd deliver.

"Thank you again, Hank."

He nodded, then turned on his heels and left.

It wasn't until later that Colette thought back over the scene with Billy Sims. She recalled the horrifying fear that had choked her as Billy Sims had leaned against her.

The fear, the horrible sensations, had all been so

familiar, something she'd experienced before, but had hidden in her obscure memories. She looked at her baby. Brook. Her sweet baby girl. Why couldn't she remember conceiving Brook? Why did she have no memory of the man who was Brook's father?

Was I raped? she wondered. Was it possible the man who'd fathered Brook had done so in a vicious violation? Was that what had stolen her memories?

"OKAY, EVERYONE, let's load up," Abby yelled to the group crowded near the huge hay-laden wagon. The evening sunshine cast golden hues on the guests and ranch workers as they climbed onto the bales of hay, their laughter seeming to hold back the shadows of approaching night.

Colette wished she could get caught up in the high spirits that infused everyone, but she'd spent the past day and a half wondering, worrying about all she couldn't remember. And she feared she'd made an enemy in Billy Sims. Abby had told her the night before that she'd had a talk with Billy, warned him that the next time he drank or got out of line, he would be fired. Abby had explained that Billy had a family, was paying child support and she was reluctant to fire him and indirectly harm his children. Colette hadn't told her sister about the frightening scene with Billy, but Hank had.

From the moment Colette had joined the group for the hayride, she'd felt Billy's gaze on her, dark and resentful. As she climbed into the wagon and took a seat, she was grateful Billy was at the front of the wagon and some distance from her.

Her face warmed as Hank sat on the bale of hay

next to her, his thigh pressed against hers. "You look like you're going to an execution rather than a hay-ride," he observed as the scent of his evocative cologne filled her senses.

"I've never been on a hayride before," she admitted, then added, "at least none that I remember." She looked toward the front of the wagon, where Billy returned her scowl. "I wish you hadn't gone to Abby about the incident. I think I've made an enemy."

Hank followed her gaze to the front. "Don't let him get to you. Billy hates everyone, most of all himself. He should be grateful Abby gave him another chance. She could have fired his butt without hesitation. A ranch is no place for a drunk."

"I'm sure you're right about that," Colette replied, wishing he wasn't sitting so close, wishing the heat of his body didn't feel so good next to hers, that the scent of his cologne didn't muddy her mind with crazy thoughts.

Maybe it's a hormonal anomaly, she comforted herself. Maybe all women after giving birth had bursts of irrational desire toward handsome cowboys who smelled nice.

Within minutes, the wagon began its trip and Abby led the group in singing camp songs. Tension slowly ebbed from Colette as one song followed another, laughter a frequent chorus. It felt good to be out with adults, knowing Brook was safe and sound with Maria at the ranch house.

By the time they got to the place where Roger Eaton and several of the other ranch workers awaited them with a roaring campfire, evening had gasped its last light and night had fully descended.

The full moon's silvery light accented the rugged terrain surrounding them. The campsite was sheltered on one side by a huge, reddish brown butte, a towering monolith reaching toward the sky. The roaring fire cast dancing shadows on its wall, creating an otherworld setting that invited intimacy.

Laughter once again filled the air as the group descended from the wagon and crowded around the warmth of the fire. The guests, four couples, immediately found seats on the hay bales the men had placed around the fire.

As Abby directed the men to begin unloading a second wagon filled with the workings for a barbecue, Colette sat on one of the bales. Roger waved a friendly hello to her from across the fire and she waved back, his pleasant smile in direct contrast to Billy's glower.

For the first time Colette saw all the ranch hands together and tried to put faces to names. She recognized Rusty Maxwell, the foreman who Abby said was her right-hand man. Bulldog had become a familiar character in Colette's time at the ranch. Although as big as a mountain, his mind was that of a child's, filled with innocence and a bigheartedness that had made him one of Colette's favorites.

Philip Weiss manned the fire, the flame's illumination playing on his grizzled features and underscoring his gnarled, arthritic hands. Colette knew Abby had been encouraging Philip to retire, but Philip refused to admit he was getting too old to be effective help on the ranch.

Bob Sanderson was a tall, thin man, his facial features tormented by a livid scar that puckered his skin from the corner of one eye to the side of his mouth. Colette knew he worked directly under Rusty with the care and maintenance of the cattle, and she'd had little contact with him.

Finally, there was Hank. Colette watched as he lifted a cooler from the back of the wagon, his biceps taut beneath the strain of the heavy load.

His gaze met hers across the expanse of the fire. A log popped, sending embers showering. It wasn't the embers that created a burst of warmth inside her. Her internal heat had nothing to do with the physical flames, but rather grew from the heat of his eyes.

She averted her gaze, wondering why it was he had the power to look at her and make her feel like he stroked the flesh of her inner thigh, breathed a whisper into her ear, knew the intimacies of her body better than she knew them herself.

"You doing okay?" Belinda flopped next to her, drawing her attention from Hank.

"Fine," Colette answered, flashing her sister a quick smile. "The guests look like they're having a good time," she observed.

"Yeah, the Friday night hayrides and barbecues are one of the most popular things we do. Wait until Abby starts telling some of her ghost stories. You'll realize our big sister missed her calling as an actress."

Colette laughed. "I can't wait."

Belinda stood. "I'd better get the steaks on. Abby appointed me the official steak cook for the night."

"Is there anything I can do to help?" Colette asked.

Belinda shook her head. "The best thing you can do is relax and enjoy the fun."

Within minutes the air filled with the scent of beef cooking over open flames. Ice-cold beverages were passed out from coolers and foil-wrapped potatoes snuggled next to the hot embers at the edge of the fire.

Colette drank her soda, isolated and separate from the rest of the group. She hadn't realized before how a lack of memory made small talk difficult. She had no past experiences to draw from, no funny little anecdotes to share. She had little else but the here and now and a myriad of confusing, indistinct half memories and emotions.

"You're awfully quiet," Hank observed softly as he eased down next to her after they'd eaten, his thigh once again a warm intimacy against hers.

"I haven't noticed you being Mr. Sociable, either." She tossed her empty paper cup into the fire.

He shrugged. "Sharing little details of my life with strangers has never been my idea of fun."

She had a feeling sharing little details of his life with anyone was difficult for him. He struck her as somebody self-contained, a man who wouldn't need to talk to or share with anyone. "I've heard from a lot of people at the ranch that you're very talented with the horses. Have you always worked with horses?"

"I could ride a horse before I could walk. At least, that's what my mother used to tell me. She ate, drank and lived horses, so they were a big part of my life when I was growing up." He fell silent, his gaze directed at the fire. "I'd forgotten how much I enjoyed this kind of work until I came here and found myself this job."

"What kind of work were you doing before?" she asked.

He turned and looked at her. For a long moment his gaze held hers and in the depths of his eyes she saw secrets, haunting secrets that again evoked in her a subtle fear...and the mysterious thrill of déjà vu. "This and that," he finally said, returning his gaze to the flames.

She leaned toward the fire, chilled by the answer that gave away nothing. He'd given the same kind of response when she'd asked where he was from. "Here and there...this and that." A kind of doubletalk that kept his secrets.

Who was Hank Cooper? And why did his mere closeness cause the blood inside her to race, her heart to thud a little faster? What secrets did he hold and why did she have the feeling that somehow his secrets were her own?

She cast him a surreptitious glance, noting the chiseled cut of his jawline, the faint growth of dark whiskers and the taut line of his mouth. He was a man who appeared to invite nothing and nobody into his world, and yet there was something undefinable, an almost primal pull that drew her to him as effectively as the cattle herd drew the coyotes.

His nearness suddenly seemed suffocating. As Abby began gathering trash from the meal, Colette jumped up to help. She needed some distance from Hank Cooper, needed some space from the heady sensations his closeness provoked.

After cleanup, everyone huddled around the fire as Abby began telling ghost stories. Colette stood to the side of the group for a little while, then drifted away, deciding there was enough horror in her own lack of memories to warrant not listening to Abby's tales of the dark side.

The cool night air embraced her, making her grateful she'd worn a sweater as she leaned against a tree trunk and gazed up to where the stars hung like jewels on the velvety night sky.

The beauty of the stars made her ache inside, an ache of isolation, the pain of loneliness. Had there ever been a man in her life who cared for her? Someplace on earth was Brook's father wondering what had happened to Colette, worried about their welfare? Or had Brook been the product of a single night of violation, a mistaken conception formed in violence?

It didn't matter. Nothing changed the love Colette had for her baby girl. No memories of violence could break the bond of love Colette felt for Brook.

"Don't like ghost stories?" Hank's voice came from the darkness near where Colette stood. He stepped closer, his features barely visible in the dappled moonlight that shone through the tree leaves.

She shrugged. "I'm just not in the mood for them."

"You shouldn't wander too far away from the group. There are dangers out here." As if on cue a coyote howled its eerie cry. Hank grinned, his teeth flashing white in the darkness. "See?"

"I'm not afraid of the coyotes," Colette replied. It was the unknown that frightened her, confused her. A lifetime gone in the blink of an eye, all experiences of love, of pain, of joy…gone, leaving behind only an inexplicable fear.

Hank moved closer, stopping just in front of Colette. With the tree at her back and him standing so close, Colette's heart began a quick rhythm. He leaned forward and brushed a strand of hair from her forehead. "What does make you afraid, Colette?"

His warm fingers evoked a heat in her as they trailed from her forehead to the side of her jaw and across the hollow of her throat. Unlike Billy Sims's closeness and touch, which had caused repugnance and fear, Hank's touch electrified her with excitement.

"What makes me afraid?" She repeated the question breathlessly, trying to keep her mind from spinning beneath the onslaught of his dark gaze and the hot caress of his fingers that still remained on her neck.

Oh, she was afraid of how he made her feel, was afraid of the secrets in his eyes, scared he wouldn't kiss her and terrified he might. "I...I..."

Whatever she'd been about to say was stifled as he dipped his head to press his mouth to hers. His lips moved softly, like a warm breeze, against hers. Someplace in the back of her mind, Colette knew she should break away, stop the kiss, but it would be like trying to rein in the wind, capture the light of a star.

As he deepened the kiss, she forgot any impulse to make him stop. Instead she wound her arms around his neck, tangled her fingers in the thick hair at his nape and pressed her body fully against his. As his tongue plummeted the depths of her mouth, dizzying sensations swept through her.

She felt more alive than she'd felt since waking up in the motel room in Las Vegas. His kiss stoked an ember of desire into a roaring inferno and she invited the flames in response.

"Ah, sweet coquette, you do stir a man's blood," he murmured in her ear.

She stiffened, something about his words pulling her away from the fire into the arctic cold of fear. What was it? Coquette. Yes, that was it. The word echoed in her head, a familiar endearment in a black fog of lost memories. Where desire had been, confusion stepped in and she pulled away from Hank. She touched her lips, which felt swollen from his kiss. "Why? Why did you kiss me?"

A lazy grin curved his lips. "Why did you kiss me?" he countered.

A blush warmed her face. "I have amnesia, I'm probably nuts and not responsible for my actions. What's your excuse?" Irritation winged through her as she heard the slight breathlessness in her voice.

He laughed, a deep rumble that again stirred something in the dark recesses of Colette's memory. "I didn't know one needed an excuse to kiss an attractive woman in the moonlight."

"Then I don't need an excuse to tell you to go away. I'd like to be alone." Colette knew she sounded petulant, but she couldn't help it. She wanted to be alone, needed time to think about Hank, and his kiss, and why his use of the word *coquette* sent a shiver racing up her spine. "Please," she added when he didn't move.

"Just don't be gone from the group for long. I was serious about there being dangers out here." He turned and walked back toward the group huddled around the fire.

Colette breathed a sigh of relief as he moved away.

Again she touched her lips, remembering the taste of him, the feel of his lips against hers.

Walking away from the tree, she headed for the far side of the huge butte, grateful for the spill of moonlight that made walking unfamiliar terrain easier. As she walked, she thought again of Hank, wondering why it was her lips seemed to know his, her body had fit into his with a familiar comfort.

Had he lied to her when he'd told her they hadn't met before? Why would he lie? Did the secrets that darkened his eyes have something to do with her, her past?

She was surprised to discover that on the distant side of the butte was a gentle rise, making it relatively easy to climb to the top. She climbed, glad for the physical activity that kept thoughts of Hank momentarily at bay.

Once at the peak of the butte, she caught her breath at the panoramic view that stretched out before her. The full moon cast luminous light across the valley, making it look like a quaint, impressionistic painting. She took a step forward, careful not to get too close to the edge where a sheer-face cliff seemed to drop into black space.

She raised her face to the moonlight and closed her eyes, taking in a deep breath of the sweet night air overlaid with the scent of wood smoke. From someplace below her, she could hear the distant laughter and murmurs of the people around the campfire.

Whatever made me decide to leave this place? She sank onto her haunches and drew in another cleansing breath. The sweet night wind whispered ''home.'' The peaceful valley below said the same. The sound of Abby's and Belinda's laughter drifting upward caused a warmth to explode in her heart, the warmth of family, of belonging, of love.

Hank. She frowned as his face filled her mind and she thought of the dizzying, tumultuous kiss they'd shared. With the mere meeting of lips, he'd made her body sing with want. She once again looked into the valley, wondering what force pulled her to Hank.

She stood, realizing she should join the others before anyone worried about her. At that moment something hit her in the back with enough force to drive her forward. In horror, she fought for balance, her feet sliding precariously close to the butte's deadly edge. She didn't scream until she realized she'd lost the battle and her feet left the butte as she plunged downward.

Chapter Five

For a brief moment Hank wasn't sure he'd actually heard a scream. It had been a faint sound swallowed immediately in a burst of laughter from the group around the campfire. Still, his adrenaline soared in response and he left the fireside seeking Colette.

She wasn't beneath the tree where he had kissed her, nor was she anywhere around the immediate area. He narrowed his eyes, trying to pierce the dark shadows that lingered beneath the trees.

Where had she gone? As he rounded the far side of the butte, he thought he heard another cry for help. Energy pumped through him as he raced up the side of the butte, stopping at the edge that dropped into apparent nothingness.

"Colette?" he yelled, his heart pounding a rhythm of panic.

"Help me, please." The sobbed request came from beyond the edge, a disembodied cry from the dark. Hank stretched out on his stomach and eased himself forward to peer over the brink.

Just below him, on a narrow jutting shelf, stood

Colette, her back pressed against the weathered wall of rock.

"Colette, it's all right. I'm right here." He kept his voice soft, hoping to ease some of her panic.

"Help me. I'm going to fall. I'm going to fall." Her voice rose in hysteria.

"No, you're not. I'm not going to let you fall." Hank maneuvered himself closer, close enough that his head and arms dangled over the edge. "Raise your arms, Colette."

"I can't. I can't move."

Hank could see her hands at her sides, fingers splayed against the side of the butte at her back. There was no way he could reach her without her raising her hands to him. "Colette, honey, you have to raise your hands for me. I can't help you if you don't help yourself."

He could hear her breathing, ragged breaths of sheer terror, knew she felt a paralyzing fear, but he had to break through that fear, get her to cooperate. "Colette, I know you're afraid, but you've got to do what I tell you." This time his tone was harsh, a no-nonsense command. "Now, raise your arms and reach for mine."

He heard her draw in a deep breath, watched with his heart pounding as she slowly inched her arms toward his. From the distance he could hear the noise of the people around the campfire, their laughter an ironic sound effect to the life-and-death drama playing out before him.

"Come on, Colette...stretch..." He groaned as her fingertips barely grazed his. Scooting farther over the edge, he exclaimed triumphantly as his hands closed around her wrists.

"Hold me," she cried. "For God's sake, hold on."

"Don't worry," Hank said, hoping...praying he could summon the strength to pull her up and over the ledge. He knew if she slipped from his grip, if he accidently let go or his strength didn't hold, she would plummet to her death.

Digging his feet into the ground, wishing for better leverage, he pulled with all his might. Within seconds his shoulders burned and his muscles shook with the effort. But inch by agonizing inch, Colette approached closer and closer to safety.

With a final burst of exertion, she cleared the edge of the cliff and fell sobbing into Hank's arms. He rolled them away from the precipice, then held her tight, too exhausted to attempt to verbally console her, but welcoming the physical contact that let him know she was safe and sound.

The burst of adrenaline that had afforded him the strength to lift her had left him and he knew he'd pay hell trying to get out of bed the next morning. Now that the danger was over, questions filled his mind. What in the hell had she done? Walked off the cliff?

It wasn't until she rolled off him and sat up, her tears momentarily subsided, that he thought she could handle his questions. "What happened?"

She pulled her legs up to her chest, then wrapped her arms around her legs. "I—I'm not sure." Her gaze went to the edge of the cliff and a violent shiver overtook her. "I think...I think somebody pushed me from behind. I was standing there, looking over the valley, and somebody shoved me."

Hank stiffened. "Are you sure?"

She frowned, closed her eyes and rubbed her forehead. "I...no, I'm not positive. It all happened so fast. One minute I was standing there and the next minute I was falling." A tremulous sigh escaped her and she looked at him once again. "Maybe I just stumbled, or maybe it was the wind. I really don't know."

As she shivered again, Hank stood and held out his hand to her. "Come on, let's get you down by the fire."

She nodded and placed her hand in his, allowing him to help her up. Together they descended the butte. "Hank." She placed a hand on his arm to stop him before they joined the people around the fire. "I—I don't know how to thank you. If you hadn't pulled me up...if you hadn't heard me call for help..." Her voice drifted off as another shiver shuddered through her.

"Shh." He pulled her to his chest. "I did hear you, and you're safe now." As Colette relaxed against him, Hank's mind whirled with suppositions. Had she been pushed? Or had she stumbled? If she'd merely stumbled, it had been an accident that easily could have been tragic. If she had been pushed, it had been attempted murder.

Hank tightened his arms around her. His blood ran cold. If she'd been pushed, that meant somebody other than him had managed to track her here to the ranch.

After several long moments she pulled out of his arms. As they walked back to the fire where everyone was now toasting marshmallows, Hank considered the men present. He didn't know any of his co-workers well, had consciously kept distance between himself and them.

It would have been easy for one of them to slip away from the fire's edge and follow Colette up the butte. Although the guests had remained around the campfire, the ranch workers had drifted from wagon to wagon and from the fire to the outer reaches of the campsite. Any one of them could have disappeared for a few minutes without arousing suspicion.

As Colette settled near the fire, Hank sat next to her. Accident or murder attempt?

He'd hoped her memory would return naturally, as she was able to deal with and process everything that had happened in the past year of her life. He feared that if he told her all of it, left nothing out, she'd run once more and this time she'd run someplace where he'd never find her again.

He couldn't let her disappear. She was a vital piece in a large puzzle.

He watched the firelight playing on her features, noting the way the flickering light caressed the curve of her jawline, emphasized the determined thrust of her chin. Desire hit him in the pit of his stomach as he remembered the hot, hungry kiss they'd shared. And mingled in with the desire was an irrational anger. Was she playing games? Pretending her amnesia for convenience sake?

Again he thought of their kiss. She'd certainly responded to him like a woman familiar with his kiss. The passion that had arced between them like an electrical spark hadn't been the kind inspired by a first kiss between two people. That instantaneous passion

had spoken of memories, of the special intimacy between longtime lovers.

Yes, he'd hoped her memory would return naturally. If it didn't, then he'd hoped to seduce her into
remembering.

If she did really suffer from some crazy form of
memory loss, then he had to walk a fine line. He
needed to give her enough of her memory back to
make her useful to him, but not enough to make her
run again. He stared at her, trying to discern what was
going through her head, how far he could trust her.

IT WAS NEARLY MIDNIGHT when Abby told everyone
to load up for the ride back home. To Colette's relief,
Billy was chosen as one of the workers to stay behind
and do cleanup. Although she had no proof, wasn't
even sure she was right to believe she had been
helped off the butte's edge, she was relieved not to
have to feel Billy's malevolent glare during the ride
home.

Hank sat next to her, not speaking, not touching,
but his mere presence eased her mind. It worried her
a little, how Hank had become a source of comfort
in her mind. He'd saved her twice now, once from
Billy's advances, and again by pulling her to safety.
But she couldn't forget she knew nothing about Hank,
only that his eyes haunted her dreams and a whisper
of memory stirred whenever he was around.

This fact, in itself, made her aware that she couldn't
trust him, didn't trust him. She had a feeling he'd lied
to her about their past association. But why would he
lie? What was he hiding?

As the wagon rumbled to a halt, Colette jumped as

Hank touched her shoulder. "I highly recommend a long hot soak in a tub for you before you go to bed tonight," he said. "Otherwise, muscles you didn't even know you had are going to scream at you in the morning."

"I'm sure I'll be fine," Colette replied, refusing to meet his gaze. She needed some distance from him, needed to sort through the myriad emotions that plagued her and she was too exhausted to even try at the moment.

She frowned as he helped her out of the wagon, his hands lingering on her hips longer than necessary. "If you need me, I've been told I give one hell of a backrub."

Heat rushed to her face at his offer. She drew a deep breath, unsure why he seemed to be romantically pursuing her, but knowing she needed to bring it to a halt. "Look, Hank, I'm grateful for all your help, but I'm in a bad position in my life. I don't remember my past, have no clue what the future holds. The kiss we shared was pleasant, but I think you should chalk it up to the craziness of the full moon. I don't intend it to happen again."

"That's too bad." His eyes glittered darkly. "When I enjoy an experience I usually try to repeat it as often as possible, and I definitely enjoyed kissing you."

She crossed her arms in front of her and eyed him with forced lightness. "Then I guess this will be a good opportunity for you to practice a little will-power."

He reached out and traced her jawline with the pad

of his index finger. ''Willpower is nice, but yielding to temptation holds a certain charm, as well.''

She stepped away from his touch, irritated with his brash appeal, with the expression on his face that subtly told her he expected to kiss her again in the near future. ''Good night Hank.'' Without waiting for his reply, she turned and hurried toward the house.

SHE GRABBED her purse and was heading out the office door when she heard the voices. Until that moment she'd thought she'd been alone. Usually she was the last to leave, always behind in her work, always playing catch-up to avoid getting fired. The voices came from the inner office, her boss's private sanctum. Moving toward the door, she strained to hear what was being said, to see if she recognized who was in the office with him.

Colors swirled and suddenly she was no longer in an office, but in a bed. And she was not alone. Strong male hands stroked her naked skin, languidly caressing each and every inch of her body. As the caresses grew more intimate, pulling her up in a spiraling whirl of desire, she struggled to see the face of the man hovering over her. A cloud of darkness obscured her vision, and still the passion grew, taking her mindlessly up...up.

With a cry, she felt herself falling...falling...into a black pit of nothingness, off the edge of a deadly precipice. And as she fell, she looked up toward the edge and there was Hank, laughing as she plunged into a bottomless abyss.

Colette woke with a gasp, her hands clutching something, anything to break her fall. In confusion she realized she clasped the bedsheet, which was hopelessly tangled around her hips.

A dream. She sank back on her pillow, waiting for her breathing to slow, her pounding heart to resume a more normal beat. Only a dream.

She turned her head toward the window where the morning sun snuck in, playing peekaboo along the edges of the curtains. Wincing, she turned over onto her side to face the window. It had been two days since she'd fallen off the ledge and still her shoulder and arm muscles relentlessly ached.

When she'd awakened the previous morning, she'd hardly been able to get out of bed. She'd finally had to confess to Abby what had happened and Abby had sent her directly back to bed for the rest of the day.

Colette didn't want to spend yet another day lounging around feeling useless, but her aching muscles told her that's exactly what she should do.

The fall was no more clear in her mind than it had been immediately after it happened. She still didn't know for sure what had happened, whether she'd imagined the force on her back or not. Nor was she any closer to sorting out her confusing emotions where Hank Cooper was concerned. It bothered her that no longer was it just his eyes she dreamed of, but rather the whole man.

She frowned, thinking of the dreams that had plagued her the past few nights. The segments had been the same…the office, the voices, the man, falling and then Hank.

Never had she had such vivid dreams, at least none that she could remember. There had been a sense of reality about these dreams that disturbed her. Were they merely her mind's imagination creating dream images, or were they fragments of memories trying to resurface?

Brook's mewling broke through Colette's thoughts and she untangled herself from the sheets and went over to the crib. "Hi, sweet baby," she greeted, ignoring screaming muscles as she reached into the crib and picked up Brook.

The baby girl immediately quit fussing and instead snuggled into Colette's body warmth. "Are you hungry?" Colette whispered as she left her room and padded down the hallway toward the kitchen. Usually Brook took a bottle immediately upon awakening, then went back to sleep for a couple of hours, allowing Colette to enjoy a later breakfast in leisure.

As she walked into the kitchen, she jumped, startled to find Abby already there. "Whew, you scared me to death," Colette exclaimed. "What are you doing up so early?"

Abby shrugged and raked a hand through her short hair. "I don't know. I had trouble sleeping last night." She gestured to the baby. "I'll hold her while you make the bottle." Colette nodded and handed Brook to her, then went to the refrigerator for the formula. "If you want to make yourself some of my special blend hot chocolate, the mix is in the container by the flour canister."

Colette shook her head. "No, thanks." She eyed her sister. "Something bothering you that's making sleep difficult?"

Abby grinned ruefully. "Bulldog has taught Cody to spit through his teeth, I can't get the books to balance, and our group of guests who left late last night took half a dozen towels with them.''

''You're kidding?'' Colette grinned teasingly. ''Cody can really spit through his teeth?''

Abby laughed. ''That's the easiest problem to fix. I intend to wring Bulldog's neck. And speaking of body parts, how are you feeling this morning?''

''Still sore.'' Colette took Brook into her arms and sat to feed her a bottle.

''I can't believe you had such a close call and none of us even knew it had happened.''

Colette nodded, grateful she hadn't told Abby that it might not have been an accident. She didn't want to add to Abby's burdens especially when she herself wasn't sure exactly what had happened on the top of that butte. ''So, what are the plans for today?'' Colette asked as Brook ate hungrily.

''Absolutely nothing. Belinda told me last night she's going into town as soon as she wakes up. I promised Cody a day of fishing and Maria left this morning for a two-week vacation. With the guests gone, I think we all deserve a day of relaxation. You're welcome to come with me and Cody to the pond.''

Colette shook her head. ''I think I'll pass.'' She couldn't explain why, but since the accident at the butte, she'd been reluctant to leave the house for any reason. She especially wasn't anxious to see Hank again. It was irritating enough that he'd so completely invaded her dreams. ''Brook and I will be just fine spending a quiet day right here.''

''Well, I'm going to go shower. If I know Cody,

the minute his feet hit the floor he'll be ready to go.''
Abby stood and carried her cup to the dishwasher.

"With Maria gone on vacation, do you want me to
do something about supper?''

"No, just do whatever you want for yourself. I
imagine Cody will talk me into heading into Cheyenne for pizza or burgers.'' As she walked out of the
room, she paused long enough to plant a kiss on
Brook's forehead, then headed to her bedroom.

Colette finished feeding Brook, then went to her
room. It was after nine when she left her room and
went to the kitchen for coffee and some toast. She'd
given Brook a long, leisurely bath and played with
her until the little girl had fallen asleep.

As she waited for fresh coffee to drip through the
machine, she noted that the house radiated an unnatural silence around her. Apparently everyone had left
for their day off. She belted the silk robe around her
more tightly, grateful that Belinda and Abby had been
generous in sharing their clothes. The suitcase Colette
had arrived with had been pitifully thin, holding only
a single pair of leggings, several oversize T-shirts and
some underwear.

Surely she'd had more things in her life in California. Where were they? What had happened to her
clothes, her personal items? What had happened to
her life?

Pouring herself a cup of coffee, she shoved away
thoughts of her forgotten past, knowing it was useless
to obsess. Obsession wouldn't bring back her memory.

After fixing herself two slices of toast, she sank

into a chair at the table, nibbling on the toast, sipping her coffee and wondering what the future held.

Would she grow old without her memories? Someday would she have to tell her daughter that she couldn't share her memories of childhood because she had none? How depressing it would be to never recover the memories of family togetherness, of happy days with her sisters, of love. How sad not to remember the man who had fathered Brook, not to possess a single memory of their union.

And what of the other memories? The ones that had nothing to do with family or love…the ones that caused a sense of danger inside her, the ones of her time in California.

She jumped as she heard the sound of a door opening, then closing. It had sounded as though it might be the front door. She stood, wondering if perhaps Abby or Belinda had returned for some reason.

Her breath caught in her chest as Hank appeared in the kitchen doorway. Clad in his usual attire of worn, tight jeans and a black T-shirt, he looked dangerously masculine. "Wha-what are you doing in here?" she asked.

"I saw your sister as she was leaving with Cody and asked how you were feeling. She told me to feel free to come in and ask you myself."

Colette stifled a groan. Was Abby playing matchmaker? Certainly the last thing Colette needed was for her sister to try to push her into a romantic entanglement. "I feel just fine, and you could have knocked before you came in."

"I did. I thought I heard you holler 'come in.'"

His look was all innocence, but again Colette had

the feeling it was another lie. And his lies intrigued her because she didn't understand the reason for them. "That coffee sure smells good, much better than the stuff we drink in the bunkhouse."

"Would you like a cup?" she asked grudgingly.

He grinned. "Why, don't mind if I do." He walked over to the table and folded his lanky frame into a chair. Immediately the kitchen seemed smaller, as if his overwhelming maleness had somehow compressed the available space.

Colette poured him a cup of coffee, then went to the refrigerator and added a dollop of milk to the beverage. She placed it in front of him, then gasped as his fingers encircled her wrist. The easy smile that had creased his features was gone, usurped by a somber, intense expression that screamed of danger. "Why did you do that?" he asked.

Colette frowned. "Do what?"

"Why did you add milk to my coffee?"

Colette stared at his coffee cup in confusion. Why had she done it? It had been automatic. She hadn't even given it any thought. She drank her coffee black. Why would she add milk to his? Because she knew with a certainty he drank his coffee light. And it was knowledge she had no way of knowing unless he'd been a part of her life before her amnesia.

She wrenched her wrist from his grip and stepped back from him, fear racing through her as she faced him. "Who the hell are you?" she demanded.

Chapter Six

He sipped his coffee then leaned back in the chair, mild amusement reflecting in his eyes. "What do you mean? You know who I am."

Colette stared at him in frustration. For some reason she was convinced she knew him. Somehow, someway, she knew with certainty that he'd been a part of her life before her amnesia. An intimate part of her life. "Is Hank Cooper your real name?"

He nodded. "It's what my mama named me and it's what's written on my birth certificate." He gestured to her coffee cup on the table. "Aren't you going to finish your coffee?"

Warily she moved to the table and slid into the chair opposite his. She wrapped her fingers around her cup, seeking warmth. Her gaze lingered on him, intently studying his bold features, the sensual mouth that had kissed her so completely, the dangerous darkness of secrets in his eyes. Familiar, so familiar. "Are…are you sure we've never met?"

He paused a long moment. He sipped his coffee, then carefully placed the cup into the saucer and looked at her, all form of amusement gone from his gaze. "Actually, we've done more than just meet in the past. We've been intimate."

Colette gasped, her mind reeling with shock at the unexpectedness of his reply. "I—I don't believe you," she exclaimed.

He shrugged. "Believe what you want." He leaned toward her, a smile curving his lips. "But it was a wild, unforgettable night for me."

Colette felt the blush that worked up her throat and swept over her face. "When was this? Where? How did we meet?" Question after question tumbled from her as she tried to fit this information into the blank spots of her mind.

"About six months ago. I was in Las Vegas for business and we met in the lobby of the Stardust casino."

"Are you telling me you picked me up?" Colette was appalled at the very idea. What on earth had been going on in her life that she would allow herself to be picked up by a stranger in a Las Vegas casino?

"It wasn't exactly like that," he said.

"Exactly what was it like?" she asked.

He leaned back in his chair, eyeing her with an intimacy that made her wish she wore something different than the thin blue silk nightgown and robe, something more substantial to ward off the near physical heat of his gaze. "We shared a kind of instant attraction. We talked for a little while, then you went with me to the crap tables. I had a couple hot runs with the dice and we laughed about you being my good luck charm. With the high of the win, we had dinner together, then ended up in your room."

Once again he leaned forward and the scent of his

cologne eddied around Colette's head, hauntingly familiar, disturbingly recognizable. His breath was warm, evocative on her face. "It was one hell of a night, Colette. The memory of that night with you is what brought me to Cheyenne."

Colette's mouth was dry, and she felt as if her nerve endings had all crawled to the surface of her skin. She was shocked at the circumstances that had apparently brought them together. But there was a certain amount of relief in hearing that they had shared a past, giving a rational explanation for her feelings of familiarity toward him. At least with this new knowledge, she no longer felt as if she were going insane.

Other, less pleasant thoughts shot through her head. "So, what happened? We spent a night together, then you left? Did you leave skid marks in the parking lot?" She was surprised by the irritation she felt.

"Whoa, it wasn't exactly like that."

"Dammit, Hank, tell me exactly what it was like." She stood and shoved her chair aside, frustration searing through her. "I've got amnesia. I don't remember things. Help me fill in some of the blanks."

She started to pace, her mind still unable to completely fit his words into reality. "Did I tell you what I was doing in Las Vegas? Did you at least buy me breakfast the next morning?"

"No, you didn't tell me what you were doing there. You did tell me you were sort of involved with somebody, but things weren't going well. I was only in town for that one night and the next morning we said goodbye and you told me if I was ever in Cheyenne to look you up."

Although at the present moment Colette knew little about herself, this kind of behavior seemed foreign, distinctly out of character for her. "So, you came to Cheyenne looking for me?"

He nodded. "My previous job ended and I decided to drift in this direction, look you up and see what happened."

"And what did you expect to happen?" she asked.

Once again he smiled, the gesture not quite reaching the shadows of his eyes. He stood and approached her, cornering her against a cabinet. "I didn't expect anything, but I'll tell you what I hope will happen." He leaned into her, invading her space. "I want to share your bed again."

Colette's breath felt trapped in her chest, making it difficult to breathe. She felt the rise of her nipples beneath her gown, as if responding in anticipation to what he suggested. "I'm afraid that's not going to happen," she replied, irritated to hear a slight hoarseness in her voice. She cleared her throat and continued, "I'm not in the habit of bedding strangers."

"I'm not exactly a stranger," he returned, the wicked smile still curving his lips. He reached out and touched the collar of her silky robe. "You did a thorough job exploring me that night in Las Vegas. You know me better than I know myself."

Colette felt the heat of his touch penetrate through the thin material, burning her skin as if he branded her. She fought the impulse to jerk away from him, refusing to allow him to see how his touch affected her.

Instead she looked at him with as much dispassion as she could muster. She wasn't sure whether to believe him or not. Although a one-night stand answered the question of why he seemed so familiar to her, why his kiss had stirred vague memories, it left dozens more questions unanswered. She simply couldn't imagine herself picking up a guy in a bar and sleeping with him that night.

She frowned as another thought entered her mind. "Six months ago. I would have been pregnant."

"Not that I could tell."

For some reason this only made her feel worse. Three months pregnant and picking up strange men. What kind of a person was she? "I think you're lying," she finally said, deciding she couldn't be the kind of person to do what he'd said. She swatted his hand away and moved across the kitchen toward the back door.

"Look in your suitcase, Colette. You have a rip in the lining and inside is a lucky hundred dollar chip. We put it there that night." He walked back to the table, drained the last of his coffee, then joined her at the back door. "It happened, Colette. And if I have anything to say about it, it's going to happen again." With these words, he flashed her one more wicked grin, then left.

On rubbery legs, Colette moved back to the table, her heart thudding the rapid beat of remembered passion. "It's going to happen again." It had been no threat. Rather it had been a smooth, velvet promise.

Although her head held no memory of their night together, her body seemed to hold the memory. As she contemplated making love with Hank, her pulse rate increased, her blood seemed to thicken and heat grew in the center of her, expanding outward like a river of lava.

But why, when she'd first seen him, had she experienced not a sensation of passion, but rather one of impending danger? Why did she get the feeling there was more to their shared past than a single night spent in his arms? And why did she still have the feeling he was lying?

She left the kitchen and went to her bedroom. Bending down, she grabbed the suitcase she'd arrived with from the floor of the closet. She placed it on the bed, then opened it. Her heart thudded as she scanned the thin blue liner, looking for a tear.

Sure enough, in one corner the liner was pulled away, allowing her hand to snake inside and find what was hidden within. Her fingers closed around a large chip. She pulled it out and stared at it. A hundred dollar gambling chip with the name of the Stardust imprinted on its face.

Her heart resumed an unnatural rhythm as a memory nudged at her consciousness. Hank lying on a king-size bed, his naked body erotically sun-bronzed against the backdrop of the crisp white sheets. "You're my good luck, coquette," he said as he flipped the coin to her. His smile faded and his expression turned somber. "And let's hope I'm yours. Before this mess is over, you're going to need all the luck you can get."

Colette frowned, reaching for more of the slice of memory, but anything else remained elusive, just out of reach. Still, what little she'd managed to remember convinced her without a doubt that there was more to her past relationship to Hank. All she had to figure

out was, what it was and why she sensed an under-
lying danger in the whole mess.

She dressed in jeans and a summer blouse, checked
on Brook, then went downstairs, her mind still reeling
with the bits and pieces of the past she'd managed to
glean. She'd just poured herself the last cup of coffee
when somebody knocked on the back door. Peering
out, she saw Bob Sanderson, one of the ranch hands,
standing on the back porch.

She opened the door. "Hi, Bob."

"Ms. Colette." He pulled his dusty hat off his
head. "Ms. Abby told me there's a leaky kitchen pipe
she wanted me to fix. So, I'm here to fix it." He
scratched the scar that ran down his left cheek, as if
self-conscious about the livid mark.

She stepped aside to let him in. "For the past two
days that leak has been an irritation. It will be nice
to have it fixed."

"It should take just a few minutes," he explained
as he set a small toolbox next to the sink and opened
the cabinets beneath. He withdrew a large wrench
from the tools. "I'll have to shut this water off for a
few minutes. That all right?"

"Fine," Colette assured him as she sat at the
kitchen table. She stared into her coffee, her mind still
sifting through the information she'd gained from
Hank.

"I guess you've gotten all settled in here. Where
was it I heard you were before?" Bob asked, his head
beneath the sink.

"In California," Colette answered absently.

"Ah, California. I lived there for a while years ago.
Beautiful state, one of my favorites of all the ones

I've been to. I was working on a ranch out there and when the job ended, I took a couple weeks and stayed right out there along the coast. Nothing like ocean air to make you feel good. Did you get a chance to spend time near the coast?''

He didn't wait for an answer. ''Yes, sir, I love the ocean. I probably should have been a fisherman instead of a cattleman. Hell, now I'm too old and too tired to change my livelihood.'' He popped his head out from under the cabinets and smiled at her sheepishly. ''I'm rambling, aren't I?'' His lips curved up in a rueful smile. ''My mama always told me I could talk the ear off a mule. Loose lips sink ships, that's what she'd say.'' He disappeared under the cabinet.

An icy chill finger-walked up Colette's back. *Loose lips sink ships. Loose lips sink ships.* Bob's words echoed in her head. Those very words whispered in her ear, a hot breath warning her as hands gripped her shoulders painfully. ''Loose lips sink ships, little lady.'' Words hissed with venom.

She stood, fighting an overwhelming impulse to run. Escape. A surge of self-protection she didn't understand, couldn't comprehend.

The back door opened and Abby and Cody walked in. ''The fish weren't biting and we got bored.'' She looked at Colette, then at Bob, who'd stopped his work as they entered. ''Everything all right?''

''Right as rain,'' Bob replied, apparently not feeling the tension that rolled off Colette. ''I've just about got this pipe replaced and that should solve the problem.''

''Good. Thanks, Bob.'' Abby directed her attention

to her son. "Cody, go and wash the worm gunk off your hands."

"I've got the water shut off," Bob said.

Abby eyed her son's filthy hands. "Go out to the shed and wash up." When he'd run outside, she took Colette's arm and led her into the living room. "You okay? You're white as a sheet and looked like you were ready to bolt out the door."

Colette drew a deep breath. "I'm fine."

"You sure?" Abby eyed her sharply.

"I'm getting little flashes of memories."

"Oh, honey, that's great. What are you remembering?"

Colette frowned. "None of it makes any sense right now. Just bits and pieces of things, but not any kind of overall picture."

"It will come," Abby assured her. "At least this is a sign that your memory is breaking loose, trying to find itself again." She hugged Colette once again. "Why don't you go outside and get some fresh air? Now that I'm home I'll keep an eye on Brook. It's a gorgeous day to be outside and you haven't really been out since your fall down the side of the butte."

Colette nodded. "Thanks, maybe I'll do just that." Walking somehow made thinking easier and she needed to think, to try to put the little pieces of memory into a bigger picture.

Fifteen minutes later Colette left the house and walked out into the bright early afternoon sunshine. In the distance gray storm clouds darkened the horizon, but she realized the rain was probably hours away. She'd have plenty of time for a leisurely walk.

As usual, her first destination was the dragon tree

in the distance. With the beginning of summer, the branches were fully dressed with thick leaves, the shape of the tree letting Colette know how it had earned its name.

Silhouetted against the backdrop of bright blue sky, the green foliage resembled a mythical dragon, complete with huge wings and long snout. She gasped as a memory whispered in her head, evoking a mental image of three little girls solemnly pressing fingers together in a ritual of sisterhood.

Every day she came here, somehow feeling if she could just sit beneath the magnificent branches, touch the gnarled rough bark, all her memories would come tumbling back. But her memories were selfish, flirting with only little pieces, sharing only shadows of scenes from her past.

She leaned her back against the tree and noticed the dirt devils rising in the breeze above the corral. Was Hank there? Working out one of the horses? Hank. She still found it impossible to believe she'd met him and fallen into his bed all in the space of a single night. But why would he lie? What did he have to gain by making up such a story? He hadn't lied about the money chip. It had been just where he'd said it would be. Did that mean everything else he'd said was true?

She sank down to sit at the base of the tree. Not only did she have Hank to consider, but also the overwhelming sense of foreboding that had followed her from the moment she'd left the motel room in Las Vegas.

She'd hoped the feeling would dissipate with each day she spent here at the ranch with her sisters, but instead it had grown. Danger seemed to pulsate in the air all around her, and yet she didn't know the source of the bad vibrations.

Leaning her head back against the trunk, she closed her eyes and immediately was gifted with a memory. She and her sisters, dressed like fairy princesses, playing house in the shade of the tree.

"I'm going to marry a prince and we'll live here forever and ever," Abby said, her face nearly hidden by one of their mother's pale white lace scarfs.

"I'm going to marry a prince and he'll be rich and I'll buy Mom and Dad a new car," Belinda exclaimed.

"And I'm going to marry a prince and have lots of babies," Colette could remember saying.

Colette sighed, remembering how filled with hope they had been as young girls, how full of romantic dreams. Abby's prince had been nothing but a drifter cowboy who'd disappeared with Cody's birth. Belinda had yet to find her special somebody who would be her prince.

Colette had gotten her wish of a baby…but where was her prince? Had she traded her dreams of happily-ever-after for a one-night stand? The Connor girls hadn't done so well in the love department.

She stood, restless beneath the weight of her thoughts. Instead of heading back to the house, she walked in a direction she hadn't explored before, away from the ranch and toward the fishing pond in the distance.

Before long she found herself in a pasture, the sweet scent of rich earth and tall grass filling her senses. Again she wondered why she had left the ranch. Had it just been an odyssey of youth? The need to escape her roots and see part of the outside world? Somehow she thought so. She could remember entertaining fantasies of what another place might hold, foolish youthful dreams of the grass being greener.

Whatever had driven her away, she knew she was now home to stay. She could easily imagine Brook running through the tall sweet-smelling grass, enjoying the feel of the ground beneath her bare feet.

She didn't know how long she walked before she realized she must have walked off the Connor property and onto the Walker's old place. The remnants of an old foundation hid among a grove of trees, only a leaning brick chimney rising upward to attest to an old homestead.

Looking up, she saw that the storm clouds were getting closer, darkening the sky to the muddy color of turbulence. Time to get home.

Before leaving the area, her attention was captured by a small bunny nearby. His nose twitched as he nibbled the sweet grass and Colette froze, enjoying the sight. He hopped toward a rise in the ground and Colette followed, surprised to see a tin-covered door appearing to lead directly into the depths of the earth. Ears raised, the bunny suddenly darted away, but Colette remained, staring at the door curiously. A storm cellar? Thick, waist-high weeds choked the area and waved in the wind that had whipped up. She fought through the weeds to finally reach the door.

Grasping the handle, she tugged and with a groan of age and disuse, the door creaked open. Wooden steps led straight down, disappearing into the utter darkness at the bottom.

She wished she had a flashlight. She'd love to explore, see what was down there. Who knew what might have been stashed in the root cellar years ago? What treasures might it yield now? There would be no exploring this time. She'd be crazy to do so now, ill-prepared for the dark.

She bent in one last attempt to see what might be down there. She heard a sudden flurry of footsteps running through grass. Before she had time to react, a blow smacked against the back of her head. A single moment of sharp pain, then darkness.

Chapter Seven

Darkness. So deep. So profound. It surrounded her when she awakened. She lay sprawled, her entire body screaming in outrage. She closed her eyes and inhaled, wishing back her unconsciousness, seeking the oblivion that had shielded her from the pain. She wanted to fall into the black void, yearned to be embraced by its nothingness. No such luck.

She'd expected green grass beneath her, the gray sky overhead, but instead she found solid earth and darkness. *Where am I?* She tried to clear her thoughts. She remembered. The blow to the head. The root cellar. She was in the root cellar.

Tentatively she moved, stretching arms and legs, checking to make sure there were no broken bones. She sat, wincing with each breath, certain that her ribs were either broken or severely bruised. A headache pounded and, reaching up, she touched a goose egg on the back of her head.

She pulled her knees to her chest and hugged them close, needing a moment before attempting to find her way back up the stairs.

Somebody had intentionally tried to hurt her.

Somebody had snuck up behind her and hit her in the back of the head, then shoved her down the stairs. She shivered as she remembered her fall from the butte. That time she hadn't been certain whether she'd slipped or been pushed. This time she was. Somebody had tried to kill her.

Why? Why would somebody try to shove her off the butte? Why would somebody try to bash in her brains? Why would somebody want to kill her? She fought a wave of nausea. Why? Why? The question made her head pound.

She couldn't think about it now. She had to get out of here. She kneeled, disoriented by her fall, unsure if she faced the stairs or away from them. Reaching her hands in front of her, she encountered nothing but space.

The sound of her breathing surrounded her. It bounced off the walls and let her know the area she was in was small. Moving her arms over her head, she stood. At least the ceiling was tall enough to let her stand. She moved straight ahead, like a blind man without a cane, unfamiliar with the surroundings.

She stopped as her fingertips encountered an earthen wall. Turning in another direction, she moved forward once again, tactilely exploring, seeking the way out.

A loud boom resounded overhead, causing her to jump and gasp in fear. Following the boom came the sound of rain on tin. She must have been unconscious for some time if the storm had moved in.

With the noise of the rain to guide her, Colette found the edge of the stairs that led up to the door. She climbed seven stairs before her head touched the slanting door. Reaching her arms up, she pushed against it. It didn't budge.

She paused a moment to catch her breath. The sound of the rain was deafening and she fought against a suffocating claustrophobia.

She tried to open the door once again, putting her shoulder into it and pushing with all her might. Nothing. Not a single inch of give.

"Help," she screamed, then realized how futile it was. Nobody knew she was here and the pounding rain would drown out what little noise she could make.

For the first time since regaining consciousness, she fought against panic. Nobody knew where she was. Her ribs shot pain with each breath and she probably needed some kind of medical attention.

She sank down onto one of the steps, the rain echoing in maddening furor. Pressing her hands over her ears to mute the loud noise, she tried to think, but one single thought held court in her head.

Somebody had tried to kill her. And if she wasn't found, they would succeed. She would die in here.

HANK RODE like the wind, the rain slicker little protection against the driving rain. His heart pounded as loud as the thunder overhead and the horse's eyes rolled in terror as lightning slashed the sky.

He had to find her. When several hours had passed and she hadn't returned from her walk, Abby had raised an alarm, asking the ranch hands to stop what they were doing and try to find her.

Hank had immediately saddled up and ridden out. He'd been working in the corral when she'd left the house and he'd watched her walk toward the distorted tree. Rusty had asked him to saddle up a couple of horses and when he'd returned from the stable, she'd been gone.

He headed toward the grotesque-looking tree, cursing the storm and his own stupidity. When he'd seen her out walking alone, he should have followed her. He should have never let her out of his sight.

Dammit. He tightened his grip on the reins, the horse protesting the heavy hand with a toss of his head.

Perhaps she'd had another snap of memory, had wandered off and couldn't remember how to get back to the ranch house. Maybe she'd slipped in a pasture rut and fallen, unable to walk home. So many maybes and perhaps.

He reached the tree, but found no sign of her. Pulling his hat down on his forehead to shield his face from the rain, he eyed the surrounding area, seeking a flash of her clothing, anything that would point him in the right direction.

To the right of the tree was nothing but flat plain and short-grass pasture. To the left, amid the waist-high prairie grass, he knew was the old Walker place. It was in this direction he headed, moving slowly, methodically, through the wild growth.

Where could she be? Surely she'd known the storm was coming and would have come back to the house if she were able. A chill stole through him, one that had nothing to do with the cold, penetrating rain.

He'd hoped she'd regain her memories here, at the ranch where she felt safe and secure. But time was running out and Hank was running out of options.

When he found her he was going to have to face some difficult decisions about her future. He grimaced, not thinking of what might happen if he didn't find her.

When he reached the old stone foundation of the Walker place, he stopped the horse and looked around. Nothing. No sign that she'd come this way. Where in the hell was she? Where in the hell could she be?

TIME LOST all meaning as Colette huddled on the steps. Every few minutes she tried once again to open the door, but to no avail. Panic became her biggest enemy, along with the claustrophobia that threatened to suffocate her.

This must be what it's like to be buried alive, she thought, the scent of damp earth sickening her. The darkness frightened her, the noise of the rain on the door threatened to drive her insane.

Despite the fact she knew it was futile, from time to time she yelled for help, until her throat hurt and her ribs ached.

She steadfastly refused to consider the possibility she might never be found, knew that to dwell on that thought would truly send her into the depths of insanity.

Somebody had to find her. Brook needed her. Colette wanted to raise her daughter, find her missing past. Her life was too incomplete for it to end now, in the bottom of a root cellar.

A sob tore through her at the thought of her daughter. A child without a father. Would she also be a child without a mother?

This thought spurred her to stand and bang on the

door once again, tears racing down her face. She screamed for help, refusing to give up as long as her voice held out, as long as any strength remained in her body.

She paused. Had she heard something? She stood still, trying to hear beyond her own ragged breathing, beneath the pounding of the rain.

"Colette?" The voice was barely discernible.

"Yes, yes, I'm here," she yelled, once again using her fists frantically against the door.

She stopped as a new noise resounded, the sound of something being dragged across the tin door. It stopped, then resumed again. There was another moment of silence, then the door creaked open.

Lightning flashed, momentarily blinding her. As her vision cleared, she saw Hank leaning down, a hand extended to help her out.

In a split second a flash of fear raced through Colette. This was the second time she'd found herself in a life-and-death situation and Hank had been the one to find her. Coincidence?

"Colette…come on, let's get you home."

She swallowed her fear, refusing to examine it at the moment. She just wanted to get out of the cellar and back to the ranch. Reaching up, she took hold of his hand and allowed him to pull her out of the dank, dark tomb.

The sky was gray and dreary, but a welcome sight to her. She breathed in deeply of the rain-fresh air, wanting to rid herself of the smell of damp earth and death.

Hank immediately took her by the shoulders and eyed her. His eyes narrowed and a muscle ticked in his jaw. "We'd better get you back to the house, then I want to hear what happened." He pulled the rain slicker off and held it out to her.

She pulled it on, although she was already soaked to the skin and chilling. With a practiced ease, he mounted the horse, then held out a hand to her.

Colette's ribs screamed in pain as she allowed him to help her up behind him. "You have to go slow," she said through clenched teeth. "I think I have some broken ribs."

As the horse started to walk, she leaned into Hank's back, fighting against waves of unconsciousness. Now that she was safe, the horror of what had happened chilled her through and through.

Who would want to harm her? Who on earth would want to see her dead? Was it possible it was the man whose body heat now warmed her? Both times something had happened, Hank had been there.

"What happened?" he asked.

"I was looking down into the root cellar and somebody came up behind me and hit me in the back of the head. I woke up in the cellar. How did you find me?" she asked, grateful that the rain had let up to a fine mist.

"Earlier I saw you take off walking. When Abby told us to see if we could find you, that's where I started."

"But how did you know to look in the root cellar?"

"At first I didn't."

She had to lean forward to hear his words before they were snatched by the wind and carried out of her hearing range. "I went around the Walker place, but didn't see anything to indicate you'd been there. Then I noticed the old root cellar. I wouldn't have thought twice about it except there were three large rocks sitting on top of the door...rocks that didn't belong there.''

So that's why she hadn't been able to open the door. Again a chill worked up her spine and convulsively her arms tightened around Hank. Somebody had intentionally placed those rocks on top of the door to keep her locked inside. An additional death warrant if the blow to the back of the head hadn't killed her.

''Colette, we need to talk,'' Hank said. But before he could continue, Abby appeared on horseback, riding hell-bent for leather toward them.

''Thank God,'' she said as she met them. ''Are you all right?'' she asked Colette.

Colette all but ignored her sister's question. She had to know about Brook. ''Where's the baby?''

''She's sleeping in her crib. Now, let's get you home.''

When they got to the ranch, Abby quickly took over, ordering Belinda to make hot coffee and insisting Hank carry Colette to the sofa in the living room. She put a call in to Dr. Washburn, then shooed everyone but Belinda out of the room. ''We need to get you out of those wet clothes,'' she said. ''Belinda, run and get the flannel robe out of my closet.''

Within minutes Colette was warm and dry, wrapped in Abby's robe and sipping a hot cup of coffee. Hank stood against the door, his gaze dark as it lingered on her.

"Now, tell us what happened. Where have you been?" Abby asked.

"I went for a walk and ended up out at the Walker place. There's an old root cellar out there. When I opened the door and looked in, somebody came up behind me and hit me in the head. I don't know whether I fell or was pushed down the stairs, but when I regained consciousness I was at the bottom of the stairs. I found my way back to the door, but couldn't get it to open."

"Somebody placed rocks on the door so she couldn't get it open." Hank's eyes held a darkness as profound as what Colette had endured in the root cellar. "Somebody tried to kill her."

His words hung in the air and for a moment nobody spoke.

"I'm calling Junior Blanchard," Abby said, rising from the sofa and heading toward the phone.

Dr. Washburn arrived and shooed everyone out of the room. After examining Colette thoroughly, he told her and the others what she already suspected. She had a bump on her head and badly bruised ribs. "You've suffered a shock and the best thing for you is rest," he said when he'd finished. "Although you're probably going to be sore enough you won't want to do anything but stay in bed for the next couple of days."

"And I'll see to it that's exactly what she does," Abby stated.

"You won't get any complaint from me," Colette replied, grimacing as she changed positions on the sofa. "I don't intend to leave this house until we know exactly what is going on."

A knock sounded at the door. ''That's probably Junior. Maybe he'll be able to help us sort out this whole mess,'' Abby said, then went to answer the door.

She returned a moment later with the tall, gray-haired man in uniform. His rugged face creased with a warm smile as he approached Colette and took both her hands in his. ''Abby explained to me about your memory loss. I didn't realize the other morning when I stopped in that you didn't remember my ugly mug. I was a good friend of your daddy's.''

''And he's been a good friend to us,'' Abby added, smiling fondly at the big man.

He released Colette's hand and sank into the chair opposite her. He took a moment to get settled, scratching his belly, then pulling a toothpick out of his pocket and popping it into the side of his mouth. ''So, what's up?'' he asked Abby.

It took only a few minutes for Abby and Colette to explain to him what had happened. Colette realized Hank was no longer in the room. He'd disappeared at some point before Junior had arrived.

Junior listened patiently, swirling the toothpick from one side of his mouth to the other then back again. When they'd finished, his smile was gone, replaced by a deep frown that wrinkled his broad forehead.

''I knew I should have been keeping a closer eye on my girls,'' he said more to himself than to anyone in particular. ''Your daddy, God rest his soul, was my best friend in the whole world, but he'll haunt my butt the rest of my days if anything happens to one of you.''

He scratched his protruding stomach once again. "Abby, I'll need a list of all the men you've got working right now. Have you seen any strangers around the place? Any vagrants?" Abby shook her head and he turned to Colette. "Have you made any enemies since coming back home?"

Colette hesitated, remembering Billy Sims's dark eyes glowing with dislike. "Only one." She quickly relayed to the sheriff about Billy's drunkenness and Abby's resulting censure.

"I'll check him out, along with the others." He rose. "And now I want to talk to this Hank fella who found you."

"I'll go with you and get that list for you," Abby said. Together they left the room.

Belinda moved to sit on the sofa at Colette's feet. "Want more coffee?" she asked.

Colette shook her head. "I just wish this nightmare was over. I don't understand what's happening. I'm afraid and don't know who to trust."

"You know you can always trust me and Abby."

Colette smiled. "That's the only thing I know for sure."

When Abby returned she was once again alone. She sank down on the chair near Colette and Belinda. "Junior says he'll be in touch. He's going to run a background check on all the ranch hands and he said for you to stick close to us until he can figure out what's going on."

"I wish I knew what was going on," Colette said in frustration.

"Colette…" Abby leaned forward in her chair. "Is

it possible when you were in California, maybe you were looking into our background?''

Colette stared at her in confusion. ''What do you mean? What are you talking about?''

Abby and Belinda exchanged a glance. ''When we were kids, we discovered adoption papers. We agreed we'd never open them, never find out which one of us might be adopted,'' Belinda explained.

For a long moment Colette stared at her sisters. The memory she'd had earlier that day. ''We…we made a pact beneath the dragon tree,'' she said.

''That's right,'' Abby exclaimed.

''We pricked our fingers and made a vow.'' The memory was once again clear and crisp in her mind. ''No. I don't think so. I wouldn't have broken that vow. Whatever is happening now can't have anything to do with that.'' She said it with the certainty she felt in her heart.

Despite her lack of so many other memories, the vow she'd made with her sisters was one she knew she never would have broken. It had been a sacred trust between the three of them, one she couldn't imagine breaking for any reason.

Colette roused herself from the sofa and stood. ''I think I'll take a long, hot bath.''

''If you want to lie down for a little while, I'll wake you up for dinner,'' Abby said.

Colette nodded and headed for her room. Once there she went to the crib, where Brook lay on her back, her little legs and arms moving as she softly cooed in contentment. Picking her up, Colette held her warmth against her breasts, needing this precious moment to usurp the dark despair she'd suffered in the root cellar.

After several long minutes of closeness, she placed Brook back in the crib, then went into the bathroom and started the water in the tub. As it filled, she stared at her reflection in the mirror.

The lump on her head seemed to have dissipated somewhat. "Who are you?" she asked her reflection. She knew her name, had flashes of memories of her life here on the ranch. But somewhere in her missing memories was the answer to who was trying to kill her.

Adoption papers. As she continued to stare at her reflection, she thought about her memory of the sister vow they had all made beneath the dragon tree so long ago.

Was it possible she'd decided to discover if she were the adopted sister? Abby told her she'd been working for a lawyer. Had he managed to dig up something about her birth that put her at risk?

She frowned. It not only made no sense, the scenario didn't ring true. She'd never wanted to know which of them had been adopted. She couldn't imagine any reason that would suddenly make that information important.

She touched a bruise on her forehead, imagining her memory locked directly behind it.

She had to remember. She had to remember what had happened in California, why she had run from there. She now realized with a chilling certainty that her life depended on it.

Chapter Eight

She awoke to a hand clasped tight against her mouth. Her eyes flew open, but in the darkness of the room all she could make out was a large bulk of a shadow leaning over her.

Instinctively she struggled, kicking out with her legs and twisting her head in an attempt to dislodge the hand that pressed against her mouth.

"Colette. Stop it…settle down," Hank's voice breathed in her ear. "I'm not going to hurt you. We need to talk." Without removing his hand from her mouth, he leaned over and switched on her bedside lamp. "If I take my hand off your mouth, will you keep quiet?"

She nodded her head. As he pulled his hand away, she drew in a breath to release a scream. Immediately his hand clamped back across her mouth and he grinned with a rueful shake of his head. "I should have known not to trust you. Okay, we'll do this the hard way. I'll hold you down and you listen."

Colette stopped her struggle and gazed up at him suspiciously. What was he doing in her room in the middle of the night? How had he gotten into the house? She moved her mouth against his palm, indicating the desire to talk.

He eyed her darkly, his raven hair spilling around his face to create shadows. "You want to try it again? I remove my hand and you don't scream? If you cooperate, we can have a rational discussion and nobody will get hurt."

Again Colette nodded. He took his hand away, but remained tense, ready to spring should she decide not to cooperate. "Rational people don't sneak into bedrooms in the middle of the night," she retorted, wishing he'd get off her.

The length of his body weighed hers down, making her conscious of the wild, evocative scent of him, the contours and planes of his lean, taut physique.

"Desperate times call for desperate measures," he answered. "Somebody tried to kill you today, and it's more than a little possible that same somebody tried to kill you the night of the hayride. You aren't safe here. I want you to leave with me."

Colette stared at him. "You're crazy. You've got to be nuts if you think I'm going to take off with you." She shoved him off her and struggled to a sitting position. "According to what you told me, I hardly know you."

"What does that matter? I can take you someplace where you'll be safe from harm." He remained seated on the edge of the bed, far too close for Colette's comfort.

She eyed him curiously. "Why do you care, anyway? If we just had a one-night stand months ago, why do you care what happens to me?"

"I'm a humanitarian. I care about my fellow woman."

"Yeah, right," Colette returned dryly.

He leaned toward her, his breath warm on her face, his scent once again surrounding her. "Okay, I'll tell you why I care." With the tip of his index finger he traced down the side of her face then paused, his finger lingering at her mouth. "I told you I want to make love to you again," he said as he stroked across the fullness of her lower lip. "I don't like people to mess with my wants."

Colette fought her impulse to draw his finger into her mouth, savor the taste of him. Her pulse rate increased, her breathing slightly painful as her bruised ribs bore the brunt. Desire beckoned, along with the sense of danger Hank exuded.

She batted his hand away, unsure whether she was more irritated with him, or with her crazy response to him. "How kind of you to worry about my welfare just so you can get what you want."

"A man's got to do what a man's got to do." He stood, as if unable to contain his energy. "Unfortunately, this isn't a game, Colette," he said tightly. "Don't you understand that you're in danger? Somebody is trying to kill you. If you don't want to come with me for yourself, do it for her." He gestured across the room to the crib. "Do you want her to grow up motherless?"

As he spoke her deepest fear, Colette got out of bed and faced him. "Get out, Hank. Before I call Bulldog and he physically removes you. I might be in danger, but I'm not crazy. And I'd have to be crazy to go with you. Now get out."

He hesitated a moment, his eyes narrowed. "It's your call." He started for the door. "For now," he finished, then disappeared out of the room.

HANK LEFT THE HOUSE as he'd entered, silently like a thief. Once outside he took up a position where he could keep an eye on Colette's bedroom window.

Time was running out. Each day that passed made danger more imminent, the stakes higher. He was going to have to do something soon. In a little more than two weeks it would all be over. One way or another. It was definitely time for him to make a final move.

He tensed as a figure loped toward him, relaxing somewhat as he recognized Bulldog's bulk. "Who's there?" Bulldog asked.

"It's me. Hank."

Bulldog grunted. "You keeping an eye on things, too?" The scent of peppermint filled the air as he stood next to Hank. "If I find out who hurt Colette, I'll kill him."

"Drastic times call for drastic measures," Hank returned. Now all he had to figure out was what kind of drastic measure he intended to use to fulfill his duty to his superiors.

"Too bad she can't remember stuff, then maybe she'd know who was after her. I don't remember stuff, but I don't have that amnesia." Bulldog pressed his hat more firmly on his head. "I'm going to walk the perimeter. I saw that in a movie one time. That's how you keep things safe...by walking the perimeter."

Hank watched Bulldog until his shadow merged

with the night. The easiest course of action would be to tell Colette everything he knew. But he knew her amnesia was a kind of self-protection and he feared what might happen if he forced her to remember things before she was ready. If he pushed her over the edge of sanity, she'd be no use to anyone.

The last thing Hank had wanted was for local law enforcement to get involved in any way. If they dug too deep into his past, they'd come up with questions that would be awkward to answer.

Yes, drastic times called for drastic measures, and the time for drastic measures was quickly approaching.

THE VOICES stopped her before she left the office for the day. She tiptoed to the door, pressing her ear to the thick wood. Who was in there with her boss? She hadn't seen anyone enter his office and yet she was certain she heard two distinctly different voices.

Words. Frightening words. Suddenly the door flew open and Colette was running. Down the hallway of the office building, aware of footsteps behind her, she ran with the knowledge she was running for her life.

"Loose lips sink ships." The words were hissed in her ear and she ran faster...faster.

Her sides ached, her lungs burned with the fever of exertion. When finally she could run no farther, she turned and looked back at her pursuer. She gasped and stumbled backward as she saw Hank astride a huge black horse galloping toward her, his features twisted in rage.

Colette hit the floor with a thud, her hands out in front of her in a gesture of self-defense. For a moment she remained unmoving in the dawn-lit room, disoriented from the nightmare that had thrown her from her bed.

Damn her mind and its relentless hold on her memory. Like a miser reluctant to share his gold, her mind released memories selfishly in distorted dreams that meant little to her.

And yet this particular dream had become a recurring one. First the overheard conversation, then the chase, finally Hank, the sequence never varied and Colette wondered if somehow the odd dream reflected something of her past.

She pulled herself off the floor, grateful to discover that although her ribs were still sore, they weren't as bad as they'd been when she went to bed.

After a long, hot shower, she studied her reflection in the mirror, surprised to find the tenderness at the back of her skull and the bruise on her forehead the only apparent remnants of yesterday's trauma. That, and an abiding awareness of danger surrounding her.

Once she was dressed, she walked over to Brook's crib. Her heart ached as she gazed at her baby who had no father. Would whomever was after her succeed? Leaving Brook an orphan?

She closed her eyes, for a moment fighting down the panic that crawled up in her throat. Maybe she should leave here, take Brook and run. She thought of Hank and his suggestion that she leave with him. How could she trust him? She knew nothing about him, didn't even know if she could believe what little he'd told her about the night they'd supposedly spent together.

No, she was better off here with Abby and Belinda.

She'd be crazy to try to run with Brook in tow, hiding from an unknown killer for an unknown reason.

After changing Brook and giving her a bottle, Colette returned to the kitchen for a cup of coffee.

''I'll never allow it. It's just not going to happen.'' Abby's voice, filled with tension, drifted out from the kitchen.

Colette entered to find her sister on the phone. ''Why now? Why after all these years?'' Abby didn't seem to notice Colette's presence as she paced back and forth the distance that the phone cord would allow.

Colette poured herself a cup of coffee, then slid into a chair at the table, wondering who Abby was talking to with such agitation. Colette wrapped her hands around her cup, thinking about her own source of agitation.

Hank. Sleep had been impossible for a very long time after he'd left her room last night. Not only had he stirred her senses on a sensual level, but he'd also stirred more questions about him and his place in her past.

Had he followed her here to the ranch? Was he some kind of deranged stalker? Was it possible he'd arranged her accidents to then be her rescuer and gain her admiration? Sounded crazy, but Colette knew the world was filled with crazy people. Her only concern was whether Hank was one of them.

Or did her near accidents have nothing to do with her past, but instead were products of Billy Sims's anger?

''And I'm warning you,'' Abby's voice rose angrily, recapturing Colette's attention. ''I won't have you messing up our lives.'' She slammed down the receiver, her entire body vibrating with anger.

"Abby?''

She looked at Colette as if surprised to see her sitting at the table. She closed her eyes for a moment, then sank into the chair across from Colette. "I can't believe it. That was Greg, my ex-husband.''

Colette looked at her in surprise. "What did he want?''

"He's planning on coming here sometime in the near future. He wants to see Cody.'' She released a short, bitter laugh. "He's decided he wants to be a daddy after all these years. Damn him.'' She jumped up, sending her chair crashing to the floor behind her. "I can't believe the gall of him. Six years without so much as a postcard and now suddenly he wants a relationship with his son.''

"What are you going to do?'' Colette asked.

Abby leaned against the counter, like a balloon deflated, anger spent. "I don't know.'' She rubbed her forehead, as if trying to ease a headache. "I just don't want him messing up Cody. Cody doesn't need Greg's broken promises in his life.'' She shot Colette a half smile. "I'm probably worrying for nothing. If Greg proves true to form, his phone call was just a momentary impulse but he'll never show up here.'' She picked up the chair from the floor, then sat once again. "How are you feeling this morning?''

"Like I was run over by a cattle truck during the night,'' Colette admitted.

"The bruise on your forehead is an attractive shade of purple.''

Colette reached up and touched the tender area.

"Yeah, I noticed when I got up. At least my ribs aren't as painful this morning. I can live with a purple forehead as long as it doesn't hurt to breathe."

"And still no idea why somebody might be after you?"

Shaking her head, Colette released a deep sigh. "None." She didn't mention her concerns about Hank, wasn't even sure where to begin to talk about him. "Whatever the reason, it's apparently locked in my head along with the memory of my life in California."

"So what are you going to do?"

Colette shrugged. "What can I do? Stick close to you and Belinda. Make sure I don't wander off by myself, and wait for my memory to return." She sipped her coffee thoughtfully. "I'd say whoever is after me apparently wants my death to look like an accident. Otherwise, why not just shoot me? I mean, I was out in the open and nobody else was around. Why hit me in the back of the head and push me down a set of stairs into a root cellar, why not just kill me?"

"But what about the rocks Hank found on top of the cellar? Those would certainly attest to the fact that somebody didn't want you to get out."

"Who knows? Maybe whoever did it intended to come back in a couple of days and move the rocks. Without those rocks, nobody would have known I was down there." Colette shivered, thinking what might have happened had Hank not found her. "Abby..." She reached across the table and took one of Abby's hands in hers. "I want you to make me a promise."

"Anything."

"If anything happens to me, promise me you'll raise Brook."

Abby snatched her hand back, obviously horrified. "Nothing is going to happen to you," she said emphatically. "Belinda and I are going to watch your back and Junior will find out who is responsible."

"Junior." Colette smiled as she thought of the gray-haired sheriff. "Is that really his name?"

Abby nodded. "Apparently when he was born, his father and mother wanted him named after his father, then decided that everyone would probably call him Junior, so why not name him that instead. It's a story he likes to tell. I know you don't remember this, but he and Dad were always close. Junior was here about everyday when we were growing up. He was like a favorite uncle. He's been a wonderful support since Mom and Dad died."

"I just hope he's a good sheriff and can help me. Until we know who's after me I'm going to be living like a prisoner, afraid to leave the house." Colette frowned. "Maybe I should go someplace else until I get my memories back. I'd never forgive myself if I brought danger to you and Belinda."

"Don't talk nonsense," Abby replied. "There has been nothing to indicate anyone is in danger but you, and the place for you is right here with us. Now, no more of that kind of talk." Abby stood. "And now I've got to get busy. Greg's phone call gave me a dose of aggression I'd better vent doing something constructive. Besides, I need to check on a horse about ready to foal. I'll see you later."

She started out the back door, then hesitated. "Belinda's already out for the day and I'm going to tell Bulldog to keep an eye on the house. He's not real bright, but he'd turn himself inside out to keep all of us safe. He'll see that nobody gets in who doesn't belong in. Keep the doors locked while you're here alone.''

Colette nodded, immediately feeling alone and vulnerable as her sister left the house. The thought of sitting around waiting for something to happen filled her with a combination of insecurity and frustration. She had a feeling she'd never been one to just sit and patiently wait.

Going back up to her room, she grabbed the sheet of paper Abby had written for her that contained the names of the men who'd recently started to work at the ranch. She was certain one of them was the person trying to kill her.

Once again in the kitchen, she sat at the table, the list in front of her. Roger Eaton. It was hard to imagine that behind his friendly smile and open face might lurk the mind of a killer. Still, what face did a killer wear?

She frowned as she studied the next name. Philip Weiss. Surely he was too old to be a killer? And yet she knew it hadn't taken much strength to shove her off the butte or smack her in the back of the head.

Billy Sims. Certainly he was physically capable of anything and his demeanor made him the most likely suspect. Still, it wasn't the open hostility that frightened Colette, it was the fear that somebody wearing a smile intended her harm.

Bob Sanderson. The rambling plumber and Rusty's right hand. Was it possible he'd come in with the

intention of harming Colette and his intentions had
been stymied by Abby and Cody's sudden reappear-
ance?

Certainly he'd said words that had recalled fear in
her, but it had been a common enough phrase. *Loose
lips sink ships.*

Finally she stared at Hank's name. Hank Cooper.
One-night lover or accomplished liar? She wished she
knew what to believe about him. His kiss had stoked
a fire of desire deep within her, but she couldn't deny
that he also created in her a vague sense of threat.

From the first instant she'd seen him, while in the
throes of labor pains, she'd had the distinct impression that rather than escaping danger, she'd run directly into the arms of danger. Why? Why were her
feelings for Hank so ambiguous?

By the time Abby and Belinda showed up for
lunch, Colette was no closer to understanding the
mess she was in or her strange feelings toward Hank.

Throughout the noon meal both Abby and Belinda
appeared distracted. Abby's gaze wandered time and
time again to her son, and Colette knew her sister was
worrying about Greg's threat to become a part of
Cody's life.

Would Colette one day face this same sort of dilemma? Someday would she get a phone call from
the man who'd fathered Brook, and would he demand
a place in the little girl's life?

Who was he? Who was Brook's father? Had he
been a co-worker at the law firm? Had Colette loved
him? She couldn't imagine sleeping with a man she
didn't love.

Her face burned as she thought of Hank. If what

he'd told her was true, love had had nothing to do with them falling into bed with each other.

"Abby, what was the name of the law firm I worked for in California?" she asked as they finished eating.

Abby frowned a moment. "Washer, Brakeman and Collins...no Collier. Washer, Brakeman and Collier. You worked mostly for Cameron Collier. Why?"

Colette shrugged. "I was hoping the name would jog something in my memory."

"And does it?"

Colette shook her head and sighed. "Maybe while I was in California a mad scientist zapped my memory permanently."

Abby and Belinda laughed. "I don't think there are any mad scientists in San Bernardino, California."

After her sisters left, Colette cleaned up the kitchen, then wandered around the living room, her mind whirling once again with questions that had no answers.

Was it not logical to assume that perhaps all her present problems—the amnesia, the threats—everything stemmed from something to do with her work?

Before she could change her mind, she grabbed the phone and dialed for California information. A moment later, armed with the number of the Washer, Brakeman and Collier law firm, she gripped the receiver tightly and dialed.

"Washer, Brakeman and Collier," a pleasant female voice answered.

For a moment Colette was struck dumb, unsure how to respond, what to say.

"Hello?"

Colette drew in a deep breath. "Hello, my name is Colette Connor."

"Colette! It's Marcia. Where are you? How are you? Gosh, girl, I've missed you around here so much."

It was obvious Marcia and Colette had been friends. Again Colette was unsure how to answer, what to say, and she cursed her lack of memories one more time.

"Where are you, Colette? That's been one of the big mysteries around here."

Colette nearly laughed. Marcia knew nothing about mystery. Mystery was having somebody try to kill you and not knowing who or why. "I'm with my family," she finally answered, strangely reluctant to give her exact whereabouts.

"So what happened? Why did you just take off? I went by your apartment several times, but you were never there. The last time I went I found out it had been rented to somebody else."

After a moment of hesitation, Colette told Marcia about her amnesia. "Marcia, you've got to help me. Was I working on something sensitive before I disappeared? Was I in some kind of trouble that you knew about?"

"Gosh, Colette, you and I were pretty good friends while you were here. We'd just gone out to dinner together two nights before you disappeared. If you were in trouble you didn't tell me about it, and I can't imagine any case that you would have been working on that might have put you in danger. But, Mr. Collier would know more about the cases you were working on."

Colette rubbed her forehead, frustration producing a slight thudding headache. "Marcia, did anything unusual happen on the last day I worked in the office?"

"You decided to work late, that wasn't unusual. At lunch that day you told me you were going to work extra late to try to get caught up on things. You were worried about getting fired."

Colette's headache blossomed. She'd been working late when she'd heard the voices. Suddenly her dream made sense and adrenaline flooded through her as she realized she was one step closer to discovering why she was in danger.

"Colette, why don't you talk to Mr. Collier? He's been worried sick about you since you disappeared."

"Okay, sure."

As she waited for Marcia to connect her with her boss, her hands grew damp with perspiration and another surge of adrenaline flooded through her. Maybe Cameron Collier would know if she had been working on a volatile case.

"Colette," a raspy masculine voice said.

Colette froze. *Hang up,* a voice screamed in her head. *Just hang up.* But she couldn't. She remained frozen, unable to do anything but breathe into the receiver.

"Colette, I know you're there. Listen, come back to California and we can talk. I'm a reasonable man. We can work this out so everything is fine. All you need to do is come and talk to me."

Colette slammed down the phone, her heart beating with the fury of fear. That voice. His voice. The last time she'd heard it was when he'd whispered in her ear. "Loose lips sink ships." His voice was smooth as oil, and filled with evil. Loose lips sink ships... what did it mean?

Was he behind the threats on her life? Why? Why could he possibly want her dead? And where did Hank fit in to all this?

"Come back to California and we can work this out," Mr. Collier had said. But Colette knew with gut instinct that if she were to return to California, she'd wind up dead.

She shivered. Cameron Collier might be behind the threats on her life, but he wasn't the direct instrument of death. No, somebody on the ranch was that instrument and Colette knew she wouldn't be safe, no matter where she was, until she found out who that was.

"IT'S ME," the man said into the phone.

"What in the hell is going on out there?"

The cowboy winced, unsurprised by Cameron Collier's anger. "She has nine lives."

"We're running out of time and I want her dead. Change her luck. Forget trying to make it look like an accident. Just do what needs to be done." Collier hesitated. "Maybe I should send a couple of my boys out on this. I thought you were the one for this job. Your record is clean, no discernible ties to me, but I must confess, I'm beginning to question your competence."

The cowboy gripped the phone receiver tightly. "That won't be necessary. No need to get anyone else involved in this. I told you I can handle it." He hung up the receiver, anger narrowing his eyes. He touched the gun that nestled inside his waistband.

He didn't want anyone else to do this particular job. He wanted it for himself, wanted the exquisite pleasure of paying her back.

Again he narrowed his eyes and scratched his cheek thoughtfully. She wouldn't be so lucky next time. She was one cat he intended to skin.

Chapter Nine

"I don't understand. Why would your boss hire somebody to kill you?" Abby asked. The three sisters sat at the table, the early morning light streaming into the kitchen windows.

There had been no opportunity the night before for Colette to tell her sisters about her phone call to the law firm where she used to work. "Who knows? Maybe I filed something in the wrong place or made too many typing errors," Colette said with an attempt at humor. Brook wiggled in her arms, as if protesting the conversation. Colette rocked her and the baby fell back asleep.

"Hmm, I've always considered that grounds for murder," Belinda replied. "Seriously, Colette, do you really think this Cameron Collier has hired somebody to harm you?"

"I'm sure of it. The minute I heard his voice on the phone I remembered him verbally threatening me." She shivered as she remembered the hissed words, the venom that had accompanied them.

"But it just doesn't make any sense," Belinda said. "Maybe it's all a big misunderstanding of some kind.

Maybe you should go back to San Bernardino and talk to this man.''

Colette shook her head vehemently. ''No, there's no way to misunderstand me being shoved down the root cellar stairs and off the side of the butte. I know somebody is trying to kill me, and I know Cameron Collier is behind it all. The last thing I want to do is return to California and confront the man.''

''I'll call Junior later and tell him what you think. Maybe he can find a connection between this Cameron Collier and one of the ranch hands.''

For the first time since arriving at the ranch, a burst of optimism bubbled inside Colette. Surely Junior could investigate the background of all the men on the ranch and find the California connection. All she had to do was lay low and wait for Junior to arrest the guilty party.

Once again when Abby, Cody and Belinda left the house for the day, Bulldog was installed as a sort of outdoor guard. Colette wandered the interior of the house, frustrated by her enforced imprisonment yet not eager to venture out and tempt fate.

After lunch, once again alone in the house, she placed Brook on a blanket in the middle of the living room floor and stretched out beside her. It was amazing how each day Brook changed, transforming from newborn to infant in the blink of an eye. Her ebony hair had grown since her birth, sleekly covering her scalp like a cape of soft down. Her cheeks had filled out to give her a cherub look.

''Where's your daddy, little girl?'' Colette asked softly, rubbing the sweet softness of Brook's cheek. ''He's missing so many things.''

Colette closed her eyes, suddenly remembering the dream she'd experienced just before waking that morning. Unlike the recurring nightmare, this dream had warmed her and caused an ache of bereavement to sweep through her when she'd awakened.

She'd dreamed of being in strong, protective arms, the warmth of a male body snuggled spoon fashion around her back. She'd felt a sense of belonging, a rightness in being in his arms, and she'd known the man holding her was Brook's father, Colette's prince.

She'd awakened to a sense of deep loss, to loneliness and fear. Where was that man now? Why wasn't he here with her and Brook, protecting them, loving them?

She had a boss she suspected had hired somebody to try to kill her, another man who professed to have slept with her a single night and blatantly stated he intended to do so again. But where was the man she'd dreamed about? Someplace there was a man she'd loved and trusted. Where could he be? Why wasn't he here with her? What possible turn of events had cast him from her life?

The front door opened and Belinda flew in. "The horse is having a bad time, the foal isn't turned right and we can't get it turned. I'm supposed to call the vet."

She raced to the phone and quickly dialed a number. She explained the situation to whomever answered the phone then hung up again. "Don't worry about doing anything for supper," Belinda told Colette as she headed back toward the door. "This could take a while."

When Belinda left, Colette went to the front window and looked out toward the barn, where a flurry of activity seemed to be taking place. Ranch hands walked in and out, their long strides purposeful.

On the front porch, Bulldog leaned against the railing, his moon face wistful as he gazed toward the barn. Assigned to stand guard, he was missing the drama of the foal's birth, but Colette knew he wouldn't shirk the duty Abby had handed him by leaving his post.

A surge of affection for the big man swept through Colette. Other than her sisters, Bulldog was the one person Colette trusted implicitly.

Sitting back down next to her daughter, again Colette thought of the predicament she was in...haunted by lost memories and hunted by an unknown killer.

It would be so much easier to deal with everything if she only knew why. Why did somebody want her dead? Why had her boss threatened her? It was all so confusing.

She froze, head tilted as she thought she heard the sound of a door clicking shut. It had come from the kitchen. The faint noise was immediately followed by the high-pitched creak of footsteps across the wooden floor.

Someone's in the house. The words reverberated through her head. Somebody had managed to get in the locked back door and was now making their way across the kitchen. The furtiveness of the footsteps chilled her.

Without thought, functioning only on pure adrenaline and primal instinct, Colette scooped Brook into her arms and ran for her room.

"Damn, damn," she swore as she realized the bedroom door had no lock. She pressed her ear against the door and heard the faint but unmistakable sound of footsteps coming closer...closer.

Panic swept over her, through her. She placed Brook in the crib, then ran to the large dresser. With a surge of strength she knew she'd never attain again, she shoved the dresser across the doorway.

She tried to still her ragged breathing, stop the frantic pounding of her heart so she could hear what danger might approach. She held her breath, but heard nothing.

Perhaps she'd overreacted. Maybe she'd only imagined she'd heard the door close softly, the furtive footsteps sliding across the floor.

A burst of hysterical laughter threatened to erupt out of her. It was probably the wind, or the old house creaking with age. When Abby and Belinda returned to the house they would all laugh about Colette's overreaction.

Any hint of laughter disappeared as she saw the doorknob turn. The door cracked open only a sliver before banging into the barrier of the dresser. "Who's there? What do you want?" Colette cried, throwing herself against the dresser as an additional barricade.

Nobody answered. The door banged into the dresser again, this time with more force. Although she knew it was crazy, she felt the venom, the malevolence, emanating through the door.

Bang. Bang. Bang. With increasing fierceness the door slammed into the piece of furniture. Colette screamed, torn between the need to run to the window and yell for help or maintain her position, adding her weight to fortify her makeshift barrier.

Several more times the door banged into the dresser, then silence. The silence seemed louder than the banging as it stretched endlessly on. Colette remained with her weight against the dresser, wondering…waiting.

What was happening? What was he doing? Was he still there, waiting for her to relax and move the dresser away from the door? Waiting for her to venture out? She was no fool. There was no way she'd do anything until she heard Abby or Belinda outside her door.

As the silence stretched, perspiration dampened Colette's hands and tickled her scalp. What was happening? She looked toward the window, wondering if she could get there and yell for help before another assault came at the door.

Afraid to move, yet afraid not to, she left the dresser and reached the window. Throwing back the lacy curtains, she unlocked it. Before she could pull it open, there was a ping and the glass exploded.

HANK HAD BEEN KEEPING one eye on the house as everyone else's attention was focused on the mare and the difficult birth. He knew with well-honed instincts that if somebody were to go after Colette, it would happen when everyone else was busy elsewhere.

When he heard the telltale ping, he knew with certainty what he had just heard was the sound of a silenced gunshot. Without hesitation, he ran toward the house.

Rather than going to the front door where Bulldog sat in one of the wicker chairs on the porch, Hank headed for the back door.

His blood ran cold as the doorknob turned easily beneath his grasp. Unlocked. What the hell good did it do to post a guard at the front door and leave the back one unlocked?

It took him only a moment to realize Colette wasn't in the kitchen, nor was she in the living room. He raced toward her room, his thoughts whirling as he ran.

He'd been the only one standing outside the barn. Apparently he'd been the only one to hear the muted gunshot. If the killer had decided to use a gun, then the gloves were off and the level of the game had changed from dangerous to deadly.

He reached Colette's door and tried to open it, grunting in surprise as the door slammed into something he couldn't see.

"Colette," he yelled. Was he too late? Had the gunman shot her? "Colette, are you in there?" He banged on the door, urgency sweeping all other thoughts from his head.

He gasped in relief as he heard a sob from behind the door. Another ping resounded. Colette screamed, and Hank hit the door with his shoulder summoning adequate force to wrench it open wide enough for him to crawl through.

Immediately he took in the scene before him, relief sweeping through him as he saw Colette curled up in a corner, crying but apparently unharmed. The baby was in the crib, arms and legs waving in agitation.

Crawling on the floor Hank made his way to the crib and picked up the baby. "Come on, Colette, we've got to get out of here." Keeping lower than the window, with the baby gripped against his chest, Hank started back toward the door.

He turned only long enough to see Colette following, then wiggled through the space of the open door and out into the hallway.

As Colette fell into the hall, another shot pinged off the bedroom wall behind her. She screamed and put her hands over her ears, as if muting the sound might lessen the danger.

"Come on. Let's go." Hank stood, grabbed her hand and pulled her to her feet. "This way," he said as he headed down the hallway back toward the kitchen.

He could tell Colette was dazed with shock. She stumbled along beside him, passive as a bewildered child until they got to the back door, then she balked. Her eyes widened. "No...we can't go out there. Somebody has a gun. We'll get shot." She stopped in her tracks. "Oh, God, what are we going to do?"

"Colette, we have to get away from here. Right now we need to put some distance between you and this ranch. And we need to hurry, before whoever is shooting realizes we're no longer in your bedroom."

He didn't give her a chance to argue or balk again. He ran out the back door, knowing she would follow as long as he had the baby. Sure enough, after a split second hesitation, Colette fell in behind him. Hank led her around to the back side of an old shed, where his car awaited him.

He got in and motioned Colette to the passenger side. As she slid in, he handed her the baby, started the engine and pulled out.

He didn't follow the drive around the front of the

house, but rather took off across the pasture, knowing once they got on the other side of the grassland they'd hit the main road.

He'd hoped she'd remember before now. He'd hoped her memory would return and she would willingly do what needed to be done. Worse case scenario: he'd hoped to seduce her into trusting him, willingly going with him. Now it was too late to hope. Too late to do things the easy way.

"You okay?" he asked. "The baby all right?"

"Yes. We're fine." Her voice held a faraway, hollow quality. "I just don't understand any of this."

"I know. I'd hoped—" He broke off, unsure what to say.

Tightening his grip on the steering wheel, he shot a glance to Colette. She had the baby cuddled close to her chest, but still appeared dazed, numbed by the entire experience. Her face was chalk white, her eyes huge as she stared blankly straight ahead.

Good, he thought. The last thing he needed at the moment was hysterics. Kidnapping hadn't exactly been in his master plan, but all the ingredients had been handed to him for a perfect kidnapping. He looked at her again, wondering what her reaction would be when she realized she was his prisoner.

COLETTE STARED unseeing out at the passing scenery, her mind replaying those terrifying moments when the window had exploded in front of her and she realized somebody had shot at her.

No longer was her death meant to look like a tragic accident. There was no way to make a bullet appear to be accidental.

She shivered and hugged Brook tighter. What if one of the bullets had ricocheted off the walls and hit the baby? Apparently whoever had been shooting at her hadn't cared, and that thought chilled her throughout.

Beneath the fear, beyond the terror of what might have happened, a surge of anger rippled through Colette. Why was this happening to her? No matter what she might have done, what could warrant these repercussions? Why would somebody want to kill her so badly they wouldn't care if an innocent baby got caught in the crossfire?

Slowly, she began to pull herself away from her inner thoughts and focused out the window. They were traveling down the highway that led toward the city of Cheyenne.

"How did you know?" she asked. "How did you know I was in trouble?" She knew Hank couldn't have been the one shooting at her, but why was he always around when she found herself in danger?

He kept his gaze divided between the highway in front of them and the rearview mirror. "I was standing outside the barn and heard the sound of a shot. I knew with all the activity in the barn it was a perfect opportunity for somebody to try to get at you."

"Whoever it was, they got into the house first." Thank God she'd heard the muffled sound of the kitchen door clicking shut. If she hadn't...if she hadn't grabbed Brook and run to her room, she knew without a doubt Abby and Belinda would have discovered her body in the middle of the living room floor. "Whoever it was, I heard them come in and I grabbed Brook and ran to my room. I didn't know what else to do."

"That was quick thinking. I'm sure it saved your life."

She looked at him, searching his face. Lines of tension cut across his forehead, slashed down his cheeks, only adding to his brutal attractiveness. "Hank, do you know what's going on? Do you know why this is happening to me?"

"We'll talk later." His gaze was intent on the rearview mirror.

"Are we being followed?" Colette asked, turning around to peer behind them. She saw nothing.

"I'm not sure. We'll drive for a little while to make sure nobody is following us. These people mean business and now the gloves are off."

Again she focused back on him. "Maybe we should go back. Everyone will wonder what happened. Abby and Belinda will be wild with fear. I'm sure Abby has called the sheriff by now. Surely he can straighten all of this out."

Hank didn't answer.

His silence filled Colette with a strange, gut-wrenching dread. She had the feeling she'd somehow jumped from the hot skillet into the roaring fire. "Hank? You need to take me back home." She heard the desperation heavy in her voice, the slight tremor that spoke of a near loss of control. "Abby and Belinda will be worried sick about me. We need to tell the sheriff what happened, let him deal with it."

"We aren't going back, Colette."

She stared at him, wondering if her recent trauma

had somehow affected her hearing. "What do you mean? Of course we're going back."

He shook his head. "No, Colette. You're going to have to trust me."

"Trust you? I don't even know you," she exclaimed, the dread exploding into full-fledged panic. She swallowed hard, refusing to give in to the hysteria that beckoned her. "If you aren't taking me back to the ranch, then just where do you think you're taking me?"

He hesitated a moment, then turned and looked at her, his eyes dark with secrets. "California. I'm taking you back to San Bernardino."

Chapter Ten

She stared at him in horror. California? Was it possible Hank worked for Cameron Collier? That he was a hired hand paid to return Colette to the man who apparently wanted her dead?

Half blind with panic, she fumbled to open the passenger door, needing to run, escape from him. With a hissed curse, he reached across the seat and grabbed her arm.

"What are you trying to do, kill yourself? Or maybe you think you can jump from a speeding car with a baby in your arms and both of you will be just fine?"

As if on cue, Brook began to wail. Colette released her hold on the door handle and hugged the baby tight. Oh, God, he was right. She swallowed hard against the panic, realizing that for the moment she was helpless to do anything to change what was happening. She couldn't risk jumping from the car and he didn't seem to be in the mood to pull over and let her out.

Her mind whirled, more clear than it had been in hours. California was a long way from here. If she bided her time and was patient, an opportunity for escape would surely present itself.

She stroked Brook's dark hair, her gaze divided between the baby in her arms and the man driving the car. Why hadn't she suspected he might be more than he appeared? Why hadn't she been more wary of his sensual charm, his seductive behavior?

Beneath his harsh good looks, she now recognized a steely strength that could only radiate from a cold, hard heart. She'd tasted the warmth of his kiss without realizing the bitterness of cold calculation that hid beneath.

Damn her for being a fool. She'd reacted to him as a female when she should have responded with more wariness. "Why are you taking me to California? Do you work for Cameron Collier?"

His dark gaze shot to her. "How do you know Cameron Collier? Is your memory returning?"

"No. Abby told me I was working for him in California and yesterday I called his office. So, do you work for him or not?"

"No, Colette." He turned and flashed her a tight smile. "I'm one of the good guys."

One of the good guys? Then why were his eyes filled with such secrets? Why did she get the feeling he spoke only half-truths? And why, oh, why, if he was a good guy did something about him still cause a responding sense of dread, of deep betrayal in her?

"I think the best thing to do is find a motel to hole up in for the night, then we can take off fresh in the morning," he said more to himself than to her. "Once we get settled in someplace, I'll explain everything to you, but at the moment you'd better buckle up your seat belt because I think we've got a tail."

Colette whirled around in the seat and looked behind them, where a car sped toward them, road dust whirling from the tires. The car was still too far away for her to discern make or color, but it was gaining fast. She hurriedly buckled her seat belt, wishing there was a car seat for Brook.

Hank pressed on the gas pedal, his knuckles white as his entire body tensed. Colette could almost feel the adrenaline flooding through him, radiating off him as the car behind them came closer...closer. It was now close enough that she could tell it was a dark blue sedan, but too far away to see the driver. "Do you recognize the car?" she asked.

He shook his head. "No. But that doesn't mean anything. There are a dozen places on the ranch it could have been parked and nobody would have seen it."

"Maybe he's just in a hurry and wants to pass us," she said optimistically. "Maybe you're being paranoid and he has nothing to do with us."

"I don't think so. Get down." The last two words were a staccato command accompanied by him pulling her head and shoulders down in the space between them on the seat. At the same moment Colette heard a sound like the crack of backfire.

She squeezed her eyes tightly closed, realizing the sound was gunfire. She screamed as the car careened, throwing her first against the passenger door, then hard up against Hank's thigh.

Brook stopped crying, apparently lulled by the crazy back and forth motion of the car. For a moment the only sounds were the roar of the car engine, Hank's steady breathing and Colette's heartbeat pounding in her ear.

Colette refused to believe her life would end here, on a narrow two-lane highway, never knowing the father of her child or the reason for her death.

"If we can just get into the city, we can get lost amid the other traffic. Out here we're sitting ducks," Hank said, then muttered a curse as another shot rang out.

"If you haven't passed it yet, there's a road on the left that's a shortcut into Cheyenne. It's right after a big white house with a mailbox that looks like a barn. The road looks like nothing more than a cow path, but it's a straight shot into the center of Cheyenne."

Hank shot her a suspicious look. "How do you know that?"

How did she? She had no idea. "I don't know, it's one of the crazy things I do remember. Believe me, Hank. At the moment the guy behind us with the gun is a much bigger problem than you are. Why would I lie about the road?"

He didn't answer. "If we can just keep far enough away from him, he can't do much damage. In a little while it will be dark and that will work in our favor."

He was right. Colette hadn't realized the golden hue of twilight had deepened to the purple shadows of dusk's last gasp. She prayed for the sweet darkness of night in which to hide.

First she and Hank would hide from the man with the gun, then once that danger had passed, she and Brook would hide from Hank.

HANK YANKED the wheel for a hard left when he spotted the road Colette had told him about. He grunted in satisfaction as he saw that the car behind them didn't make the turn. Good. Although he knew their pursuer would quickly right his error, even a moment of time might give them the lead they needed to evade him.

He only hoped Colette hadn't been foolish enough to lie to him about where this particular road led. He looked down to where Colette was still hunched, half lying on the seat next to him, her head pressed against his thigh.

Her hair was a chestnut spill against his faded blue jeans and her perfume filled the interior of the car. Despite the tenseness of their predicament, Hank felt a stir of desire.

He gripped the steering wheel more tightly, fighting down the emotion. It had been his selfish lust that had gotten things so screwed up in the first place. He didn't intend to make the same mistake again.

He'd always been very good at control, and he intended to maintain tight control on himself and the situation until Colette's role in this particular drama was over. Then he'd walk away, as always unscathed and alone.

Although he'd intended to use seduction to get her to leave the ranch with him, seduction was no longer necessary, and in fact would only further complicate matters.

Pressing on the gas pedal in an attempt to lengthen their lead, he glanced in the rearview mirror, satisfied that for the moment no other cars were in sight. Still, he knew for the next couple of weeks he'd have his work cut out for him.

Cameron Collier was a powerful man, with long arms for vengeance, and he wouldn't rest until Colette was eliminated. Collier would spare no expense, no manpower, to find them. For the next sixteen days, Hank knew he and Colette would find themselves the rodents in a deadly game of cat and mouse.

He breathed a sigh of relief as houses and traffic began to appear, letting him know they were approaching the city limits.

Within minutes darkness had fallen completely and Hank began to relax. "You can sit up now," he said.

She pulled herself upright and looked around, visibly relaxing as she realized they'd made it into town. "What do we do now?"

"We drive around for a while, make sure we don't have a tail, then find someplace to hole up for the night."

"Hank, please just take me back to the ranch." Her eyes were wide, glazed with suppressed tears. "I—we'll pay you. My sisters and I will give you whatever you want."

"I don't want money. Besides, with the financial state of that ranch, you and your sisters couldn't get up a decent ransom between you," he scoffed. "This isn't about money. It's about murder."

"Murder?" Colette's voice squeaked and Hank damned himself for saying it so bluntly.

"I told you, I'll explain everything when we get settled someplace for the night."

"Then you better get us settled right now because I want some answers," Colette retorted.

Yes, it was time to get settled for the night, time for Colette to get some answers. He was aware that he walked a fine line. Too few answers and she wouldn't understand her place in the scheme of things, too many answers and she'd run the first chance she got.

A lot of people were depending on her to get her memory back, but with it would come memories that would make her hate him. He'd just have to deal with her hate, he had to keep focused on the importance of the bigger picture, not the frailty of human emotions.

Confident that they were not being followed, Hank pulled into the parking lot of the Sleepy-Time Motel. "Not exactly four stars, but it will do for the night," he said. He hesitated before getting out.

If he went into the office to rent a room, would she and the baby still be here in the car when he came back out?

The alternative was to take her inside with him, inside where she could scream that he'd kidnapped her, inside where she could make a scene. The last thing he needed was anything that would draw attention to them.

He had to trust that her curiosity alone would keep her with him until she got some answers. "Once we're in the room, I'll tell you everything," he said as he got out of the car.

Colette watched him walk into the office and knew now was her chance to escape. All she had to do was find a phone, call Abby, and her sisters would come and get her. But she hesitated.

Hank had led her to believe he held all the answers

to everything that had haunted her from the moment she'd become conscious in that motel room in Las Vegas. She desperately needed those answers. If she ran now, she'd never know what, exactly, she was running from.

If I don't run now, I'm a fool, she told herself. Who knew when another opportunity for escape would present itself? She opened the car door, the noise awakening Brook, who yelled an angry yowl.

As she saw Hank returning to the car, she realized the opportunity to escape was lost. She'd taken too long to make up her mind. She slammed her door, at the same time soothing Brook. Hopefully the chance for escape would come once again.

"Room 124," he said as he scooted into the driver seat.

When they found the room, she wondered if he'd specifically asked for one in the back, where their car would not be visible from the main road.

The room was typical of every cheap motel room in every city in every state of the union. Two full-size beds covered in worn gold spreads, a nightstand scarred with stains and cigarette burns and, beneath their feet, gold shag carpeting merely added to the depressing decor. The whole room seemed to breathe deep hopelessness, abiding despair.

Colette placed Brook, who had fallen asleep, into the center of one of the beds, then turned and looked at Hank expectantly. "Okay, we're here. We're settled. Now I want some answers."

Hank kicked off his boots and stretched out on the bed, his arms crossed behind his head. His posture was unconsciously sensual, evoking a whisper of déjà vu in Colette as his dark eyes played over her.

Had he looked at her that way the night they'd supposedly had their one-night stand? Had his eyes been so sensually dark and hot, so filled with suppressed emotions? Or was she remembering another time, another man? She pushed these thoughts aside, needing to focus on the main issue.

"You told me in the car that you're one of the good guys. So, what exactly does that mean?"

He reached into his back pocket and withdrew his wallet. He flipped it open and tossed it to the foot of the bed. It remained open, displaying a badge and an identification card.

Colette picked it up and read the card. Hank Cooper. U.S. Marshal. She threw the wallet back to him. "Just because you're a marshal doesn't mean you're one of the good guys," she replied, although in truth this piece of information took the edge off her fear of him.

"True, I suppose. But in your case, I'm on your side."

Colette sat on the edge of the bed where he remained stretched out. "So, exactly what is my case?"

He sat up and plumped the pillows behind his shoulders. Colette eyed him suspiciously, wondering if he was stalling to get his story straight or if he'd merely been uncomfortable.

He settled back once again, his gaze unwavering on her. "In less than three weeks you are scheduled to appear in court to give testimony against Cameron Collier on murder charges."

Although somehow in some deep part of her his

words didn't surprise her, a chill waltzed up her spine. "Murder charges? Did I see the murder?" she asked. Certainly the trauma of seeing somebody killed would explain her amnesia. She wouldn't want to remember such a heinous thing.

Hank shook his head. "You didn't see the murder, but you heard the payoff between Collier and the man he hired. It was a contract killing."

She'd been working late when she heard voices coming from Mr. Collier's office. The dream that had haunted Colette night after night suddenly made perfect sense.

It had been her memories reaching out to her in the darkness of night, in the fragments of dreams. "I remember…bits and pieces. Hearing something that frightened me, then somebody chasing me."

"You managed to get away and went directly to the police. They immediately made arrangements to put you with us in protective custody."

"When…when was this?" she asked as she wrapped her arms around herself, fighting against an inner chill. "When did all of this happen?"

He sat up, his gaze moving from her to the baby on the opposite bed. "About seven months ago. We knew Collier would try to get to you. I was assigned to make sure that didn't happen."

"Who was killed? Who was the victim?" she asked, her head reeling.

"A city councilman who intended to vote some zoning that Collier didn't like. Apparently Collier tried to buy him off first. When that didn't work he decided to kill him."

"So what happened? How did I end up alone in

Las Vegas? How did I wind up back at the ranch?"
Each answer he gave her called for more questions.

"I can't answer that. All I know is we were in a
hotel in California. I left to pick up some things and
when I got back you were gone."

She stared at him searchingly. Although he appeared perfectly relaxed, she sensed the tension of
coiled muscles, the watchful wariness of a cunning
animal. Again she had the sense that this man could
be dangerous, that emotions like compassion, vulnerability...love...had no place in his life.

"When you turned up at the ranch, we figured that
was the safest place for you until the trial. At least
you'd be with your family."

"Did we really have a one-night stand in Las Vegas?" she asked as she stood, too keyed up to sit still.

He averted his gaze from hers and grabbed his wallet, then tucked it back into his pocket. "Nah. I
thought if I told you that you'd be more likely to
come with me when it was time for us to head back
to California."

"So you intended to seduce me with lies."

He shrugged. "Whatever it took to get the job
done." His lips curved into a wicked smile as his gaze
swept over her slowly, sensually. "Although if you
understand the rules, I'm certainly game for a little
seduction to help pass the time."

"And what are the rules?"

With one smooth movement he got up off the bed
and approached where she stood. Although her instincts screamed for her to back up, not let him get
close, her pride kept her rooted to the spot.

"The rules are simple," he said as one of his hands

reached up to stroke her hair. He stood so close to her his warm breath fanned her face and his wild, provocative scent enveloped her as he continued. "No strings," he explained, his hand leaving her hair and trailing down to the pulse in the hollow of her throat. "No commitment." He caressed her neck, his hand warm against her flesh. "As long as both parties understand the rules, there's no harm in a little seduction."

She knew the pulse in her throat throbbed erratically and her blood had slowed to a languid heavy flow. His touch was like a drug, beckoning her toward surrender as his hand moved from her neck to her shoulder.

For the space of a second she wanted to throw her head back, fall into the seduction she knew would momentarily erase her fears, quiet all questions and reduce her to nothing but physical responses. But the moment passed quickly and irritation took the place of temporary insanity.

"Is seducing those you're sworn to protect part of your job description?" She moved away from him, relieved to put some distance between them. "So basically, what you're telling me is that I'm supposed to testify at a trial and that's why somebody is trying to kill me," she said, attempting to get the subject back on track.

His eyes flashed darkly and he sat back on the bed. "That's about the size of it."

"But how can I testify without my memories?"

"There are a lot of people depending on you getting those memories back before the trial."

"And if I don't?"

"They'll hire the best doctors, try drugs and hypnotherapists...whatever it takes to release those memories."

"My testimony is that important?"

Hank raked a hand through his thick black hair, his eyes narrowed. "We've been trying to get Cameron Collier for years, but the man is smart and has managed to distance himself from every vile act he's instigated. He's powerful and evil. Your testimony is our best chance of putting him away permanently."

Colette rubbed two fingers across her forehead, where a headache had begun an insistent pounding. "I can't believe this is happening." She rubbed her forehead once again, then looked back at Hank. "What if I refuse to testify? Then Cameron Collier would leave me alone and everything would be fine."

"Except you'd be in prison for obstructing justice."

She gasped. "Surely they wouldn't do that. I have a daughter. They wouldn't put me in jail."

Hank laughed. "Don't make the mistake of thinking anyone cares whether you're a mother or not. All these people care about is putting Collier away for a long time behind bars. Besides, don't be naive enough to think Collier will leave you alone. You're marked for death as far as he's concerned."

"But if you let me go, I could disappear. Collier couldn't find me and neither could the police."

He sighed and once again raked a hand through his shiny long hair. "I can't do that. I have a job to do and I intend to deliver you to the authorities in California when it's time. Besides, do you want to spend the rest of your life looking over your shoulder?"

Colette sighed in frustration. "It sounds like no matter what I choose to do, that will be the outcome. If I testify and Collier is such a powerful man, what's to keep him from having somebody come after me even if he's in prison?" She shivered. Until this moment she hadn't realized how alone she was in all this, what a no-win situation it was for her.

"Colette, I can't make you testify. I can only tell you that before you developed amnesia, you wanted to, you knew it was the right thing to do."

"Well, I've changed my mind. Just let me go."

"I told you, I can't do that. It's my job to get you to trial, and that's exactly what I intend to do."

Over my dead body, Colette thought. She'd rather take her chances against the people in law enforcement than a killer like Collier.

She sank down onto the edge of the bed where Brook lay sleeping. "So before I ran away, your job was to baby-sit me, so to speak?"

"So to speak," he said dryly. "We were holed up together in a hotel room, mostly getting on each other's nerves and impatiently biding time."

Why didn't she remember any of it? Had the experience of sharing living space with Hank been so unpleasant she'd blocked it out along with the murder? Or was he still telling lies?

She stared at her daughter and realized a very important question had yet to be answered. He'd said this had all begun about seven months before, so she would have already been pregnant when she'd overheard the conversation in Collier's office. "Do you know who Brook's father is?" she asked softly.

He stared at her, his eyelids half mast over his dark, glittering eyes. "I don't know."

"I didn't tell you?"

"We shared a room, Colette, we didn't bare our hearts." He stood. "I'm going to have to run out and buy some things we're going to need. Tell me what you need for the kid that won't wait until morning."

"Formula, a bottle and diapers," she said, hoping, praying, he intended to take her with him.

All she needed was one minute of inattention, one second to make a clean escape from him. There was no way she intended to let him get her back to California, no way she intended to risk her life, especially now that she had Brook to consider.

Hopefully in a store she could lose him. She didn't know what she would do once she evaded him…she'd deal with that particular dilemma when the time came.

"You don't, uh, breast-feed?" His face reddened slightly.

She shook her head, also feeling the warmth of a blush. "Apparently stress plays havoc with a body. Let's go." She stood.

He shook his head and for a brief moment regret flashed in his eyes. "Sorry, it's safer if I go. You stay here." He pulled his belt off and approached her.

"Wha-what are you doing?" she asked, backing away from him.

"I'm sorry, Colette, but I can't let you run again."

She bumped against the wall. "I won't. I won't run," she exclaimed.

"Don't make this difficult." He whirled her around and pulled her hands behind her back. Despite her struggle, he managed to tie her hands together with his belt.

He scooped her up into his arms and placed her in the center of the bed where he'd been lying. As Colette attempted to get up, Hank unplugged the phone cord from the wall, then from the back of the phone and fastened it through the belt around her hands to the headboard of the bed.

"What are you doing? Are you crazy?" Colette yelled. She felt like a young steer, lassoed and helplessly tied.

"I'd be crazy to trust you," he said as he pulled a handkerchief from his back pocket.

Impotent tears sprang to Colette's eyes as he once again approached her and tied the handkerchief around her mouth, effectively gagging any of her further protests.

For a long moment his gaze held hers as he remained bending over her. His dark eyes flickered with an indefinable emotion and he reached out and gently brushed a strand of her hair away from her forehead. "I'm sorry it has to be this way," he whispered as his hand lingered on the side of her face and his eyes pierced to her soul.

Despite her anger, beyond her fear, another emotion appeared, desire evoked by his touch. It surged, as strong as a memory, as familiar as the hand that spawned it. Why? Why did the touch of his hand not only produce a swift heat of desire, but also the whisper of sweet recollection?

His eyes flashed again, this time dark and cold. He stood and moved toward the other bed. "I'll take the baby with me. A little insurance that if you happen to get untied you won't do anything stupid." He picked up the sleeping child, who cuddled against his broad chest. "I shouldn't be long."

With these final words, he disappeared out the door.

Again hot tears burned at Colette's eyes. What kind of a man was he to leave her like this? She concentrated on not crying, knowing if she did her nose would stuff and the handkerchief across her mouth would make it difficult to breathe. Although it would serve him right to return and find her dead, suffocated to death.

She didn't even attempt to get free. The moment he'd decided to take Brook with him, he'd won this particular round. But there would come another time, another chance to escape.

There was no way she was going to allow him to take her to California to testify in a trial she knew would put a target on her head. Somehow, someway she'd let Cameron Collier know he had nothing to fear from her and then he'd leave her alone.

If it was just herself she had to worry about, perhaps she'd feel differently about testifying. But she wasn't alone. She had Brook to consider. Brook needed her alive, not with a bounty on her head.

She might feel differently if she had somebody in her life to support her, somebody who could make her feel secure and loved no matter what choice she made. But she didn't. It wasn't fair to put this kind of life-and-death burden on her sisters, and she had no idea who or where Brook's father was.

She was alone...except for Hank. Hopefully he

could keep her safe until she could talk to Cameron Collier and tell him to call off his troops.

As she thought of that moment when Hank's touch had pulled forth a violent burst of desire, she wondered, as Hank kept her safe from Collier's men, who would keep her safe from Hank?

Chapter Eleven

Hank held the baby awkwardly in one arm as he pushed the cart down the aisle of the discount variety store. He didn't like the way the baby felt in his arms, all sweet innocence and pure need.

He hadn't wanted to take the baby along, but he hadn't known how else to handle the situation. The baby was an unwanted complication and an ace in the hole for making Colette cooperate.

Standing in front of the display of diapers, he tried to ignore how her sweet breath warmed his neck, how her baby powder scent seemed to sweep him back to a time long ago. A time of hope, of dreams...all shattered in the blink of an eye.

He no longer had the energy to hope, and had lost all his ability to dream. He was a man with a cold heart, and no pretty brunette with big hazel eyes or dark-haired cherub babe would change that fact.

He grabbed a package of diapers he thought would fit and shoved all thoughts of that distant past behind. Moving on to the canned formula section, he concentrated on making a mental list of what other things they might need for a couple of days on the road.

As he threw a couple of baby sleepers into the basket, Brook continued to sleep in his arm, her long lashes feathering her chubby cheeks. He tried not to look at her, didn't want to fall into the kind of love affair babies easily inspired in most people.

From the baby section, he moved to womens' wear, knowing Colette had nothing but the clothes on her back. It was unfortunate their escape hadn't been better planned. A packed suitcase of clothing and necessities would have been nice.

At least he had most of his own things. Knowing there might come a time when he'd have to leave the ranch fast, he'd kept his own clothes and personal items in the car.

He added a couple oversize T-shirts and several pairs of jogging pants to the items in his basket, then as an afterthought threw in an infant car seat and headed for the cashier.

"Oh, what a sweet baby doll," the cashier exclaimed as she rang up Hank's purchases. "How old is she?"

"Not even a month," Hank answered. He looked down at Brook, surprised to see her not only awake, but her bright dark eyes peering up at him. As he stared at her, her tiny mouth turned up into a smile.

"Look at that, isn't that precious. She's smiling at you." The cashier's voice rose an octave and a headache blossomed in the center of Hank's forehead.

"It's probably gas," he answered, wishing she'd hurry up.

"You must be such a proud papa," she said.

Hank merely grunted. He paid for his purchases, then headed for his car, hoping Colette hadn't gotten loose and done something stupid. He paused long enough to use a pay phone to call his superior and let him know where they were and what had transpired, then headed back to Colette.

Colette. As he drove back to the motel, taking side streets and alleys in an effort to elude anyone who might be possibly following him, his head filled with thoughts of her.

He'd always believed the adage that familiarity bred contempt, but that hadn't been the case between him and Colette. Days and nights of togetherness had fostered a steaming desire, an explosive passion that had simmered to uncontrollable proportions.

His control had snapped and complicated what should have been an easy assignment, complicated the lives of everyone involved.

He'd vowed to himself five years before that his heart would never be touched again, and it was a promise he intended to keep. Colette would have his protection, and as long as she understood the rules, she could even experience his passion, but she'd never, ever warm his cold, hard heart.

He parked in front of their motel room, seeing nothing amiss. Still, caution came as natural as breathing. He kept the motor running and the baby in the car seat as he got out of the car and approached the room. Pulling the key from his pocket, he placed an ear to the door.

He wasn't concerned about her getting loose and calling the local law. His authority far exceeded theirs and they would only remand her back into his custody. What did worry him was that if she'd managed to call the law, who else might have heard telltale radio transmissions? The one mistake Hank knew better than to make was to underestimate Cameron Collier.

He heard no sounds emanating from inside the room, had no whisper of danger walk up his back. His instincts all proclaimed it safe and he had learned long ago to depend on his unscientific but nearly faultless instincts.

It took him only moments to shut off the car, gather Brook and the packages from the back seat, and open the motel room door.

Colette remained in the same position he'd left her, her eyes shooting anger and resentment as he entered. He placed the baby and the shopping bags on the other bed, then quickly untied Colette from her bonds. She sat up and rubbed her wrists, her eyes steady on him. "It was enough that you took my baby with you, you didn't have to tie me up like a steer."

"If I'd thought it unnecessary, I wouldn't have done it," he replied as he wrapped the phone cord in a small bundle and shoved it into his pocket. He gestured to the packages on the bed. "I picked up the stuff for the kid, and I also bought a couple T-shirts and jogging pants so you'd have a change of clothes."

"You're so good to me," Colette returned sarcastically.

He sank down on the edge of his bed, suddenly exhausted. The past months of not knowing where Colette was, if she were still alive, or if Collier had gotten to her, had stretched his nerves.

Now that she was where she needed to be, he didn't want to fight with her. He didn't want to have to watch not only her back, but his own, as well, worrying about whether she'd run or not.

As she opened a can of the formula and prepared a bottle for the baby, Hank absently rubbed a hand across his forehead where a band of tension pressed painfully. Why couldn't she just cooperate with him? It would be so much easier if he could trust her, so he could go in and take a hot shower, then get a couple hours of deep sleep without worrying about her sneaking out and disappearing once again.

"Shouldn't you heat that or something?" he asked as she finished preparing the bottle and picked up Brook.

"It isn't necessary. The formula is sterile and room temperature."

Brook was in her arms, drinking from a bottle and for a moment the picture of mother and child caused a strange warmth to suffuse him.

Colette's head was bent, her hair forming a curtain of brown silk as she smiled down at the baby. He'd never seen Colette look so soft. It was as if the mere act of feeding her child created a peace in her that transcended any other problems she might face.

There were things he needed to explain to her, things that he hoped would make her realize she had to trust him, make her reluctant to run. But he remained silent, loath to shatter the momentary peace she'd found.

He knew he should look away from her, but like the moon pulled the tides, something about the scene drew him. As he watched, Colette rubbed a finger across Brook's cheek, then laughed and murmured something too low for Hank to hear.

He'd seen Colette's eyes filled with anger, snapping with impatience and glazed with frightened tears, but in the time they'd been together, he'd never seen her so softly vulnerable, so filled with tenderness. He suddenly felt threatened, bewitched by the heat that swirled inside him, the beauty of her loving smile.

"We need to talk," he said, his voice louder than intended, smashing the momentary quiet of the room.

"So talk." Her eyes flashed annoyance and an edge of relief swept through Hank. Annoyance was good. Irritation was good. Far better to deal with those emotions than the alien ones she'd stirred moments before.

She placed the baby at her shoulder and patted her back, looking at him expectantly.

"Colette, I don't think you fully understand the danger you're in, the fact that if you escape from me you'll probably end up dead. Until we get to California, your only hope for staying alive is to remain with me."

He raked a hand through his hair, his gaze remaining on her. "Think about it. You have no money, no memory of friends to turn to for help. How long can you survive on your own with the baby, hiding from killers?" He could tell he was getting to her. She half flinched beneath each statement of fact. "I can't tell you how dangerous Cameron Collier is. He's powerful enough to find you no matter where you try to hide."

"But my sisters—"

"You'd only place them in danger," he said, cutting her off. "Colette, you have to understand. The next two weeks are going to be the most dangerous you ever experience. You won't survive them without me. And I won't survive them if I have to watch my back with you.''

"What do you mean?" she asked, all innocence that didn't fool him a bit.

"To be smarter, better than Collier's men, I'll need sleep, and I can't sleep if I know each time I close my eyes you'll try to get away. Hell, I can't even contemplate a nice hot shower unless I take the baby into the bathroom with me as a little insurance.''

Her face flushed a becoming pink as she placed the baby, who'd fallen asleep, back on the bed. She rubbed her forehead, as if she, too, suffered a tension headache. "I'll make you a deal,'' she finally said. "I promise you I won't try to escape between here and California.''

He eyed her skeptically. Could he trust her to keep such a promise? He'd like to think he'd gotten through to her on an intelligent level, but knew Colette was the type of woman who functioned most of the time on emotions.

Yet, in her eyes he didn't see a lie, but rather saw the resignation of a woman who knew he'd told her the truth about her situation.

"Do you ever break your promises, Colette?"

She smiled. "I can honestly say I can't remember a single time that I've ever broken a promise.''

"Easy to say when you have amnesia.''

She shrugged. "It's the best I can do.'' A sigh escaped her. "Hank, I've given you my word and I intend to keep it. Besides, it's been a rather trying day and at the moment I'm just too damned tired to try to escape.'' She stood. "In fact, if you aren't going to use that hot shower, I will.'' She grabbed a pair of the jogging pants and one of the T-shirts he'd bought, then with a final check on Brook, disappeared into the bathroom.

As the sound of the water running echoed from the tiny bathroom, Hank kicked off his boots and stretched out on the bed.

Just a little more than two weeks…sixteen days and he could finally put this case and Colette Connor behind him. A year of his life had been devoted to what should have taken the justice system mere weeks. But the criminal docket had been full, and the judge assigned to the case had been lenient in granting delays and postponements to Collier's legal eagles.

Hank had been relieved to hear there would be no more delays. Cameron Collier would have his day in court, and Hank would make certain the star witness was there. Too bad he couldn't guarantee she'd remember the incriminating conversation she'd overheard. Nor could he guarantee what her life would be like after testifying.

He closed his eyes, shoving away thoughts of what might happen to her after this was all over. It had nothing to do with him. He'd continue his life… alone, his hard heart unscathed.

Despite his efforts to the contrary, as the shower continued to run, a mental image of Colette beneath the spray filled his brain. He could easily imagine her head thrown back, her lithe body thrust beneath the spray.

He knew, from the time they'd spent together before, that she liked her shower hot enough to turn her skin a rosy pink. She'd use the washcloth laden with suds languidly, beginning at her shoulders, then caressing across her full breasts...down the flat of her stomach, across the slight protrusion of her hip bones—

With a muttered oath, he pulled himself off the bed, fighting against a wave of internal heat so intense it threatened to overwhelm him.

He opened the motel room door and stepped outside, the cool night air caressing his fevered skin. Not only did he have to worry about Collier's men finding them before the trial, he also had to worry about himself and maintaining control over the crazy, powerful desire Colette stirred in him.

He knew Colette didn't understand his rules, the ones that had kept him sane for the past five years of his life. She wasn't the type of woman to enjoy their enforced intimacy, indulge in passion without commitment, sex without love. And he wouldn't have a relationship any other way.

Pulling his keys from his pocket, he walked to his car. He opened up the trunk and withdrew a duffel bag that held clean clothes and toiletry items. He took a few deep breaths of the cool night air, then went back into their room.

COLETTE RINSED her hair beneath the spray for a second time, wishing she had a bottle of shampoo instead of the tiny bar of soap the motel had provided.

As she worked to get the last bit of suds out, her mind whirled with suppositions and what-if's. The initial panic she'd felt, the horror of realizing Hank wasn't taking her home, had passed, leaving in its wake a dull resignation.

She intended to keep her promise to Hank. She wouldn't attempt to run from him between here and California. She didn't want to put her family at risk by going back to the ranch, and had no money, no place else to go.

In California perhaps she could connect with Marcia. It had been obvious when she'd spoken to the young woman on the phone that she and Colette had been friends. Surely Marcia could loan her some money, help her disappear from those who wanted to harm her. Perhaps she could even talk to Collier again, explain to him about her amnesia, let him know he had nothing to fear from her. Yeah, right. She frowned, knowing it was those kinds of naive thoughts that would end up getting her killed.

She shut the water off and grabbed one of the thin, motel-issue towels. As she dried herself off, she thought again of the man who held her captive.

Initially he'd told her they'd had a one-night stand, then he'd told her that wasn't true, that he'd lied. And yet she still had a feeling they'd been more than uneasy strangers trapped together by circumstances.

His kiss had stirred a whisper of memory, a remembered response of passion. Why? Had they been lovers? Then why would he lie? How could she completely trust him when she still saw secrets in his eyes, still sensed lies in his heart?

Still confused, she yanked on the pair of black sweatpants and the oversize light blue T-shirt. At least she was grateful he'd realized she wouldn't want to spend the next couple of days in the same clothing.

Standing in front of the mirror, she did her best to finger-comb her wet hair, wishing for a brush. She stared at her reflection. "Why can't you remember?" she asked her image.

What was it that kept her memory firmly hidden behind locked doors in her mind? What event had cast her into the darkness of amnesia? And why...why did she have a feeling Hank was at the heart of it all?

She didn't fear him physically. She knew if he'd wanted to harm her, he'd had a dozen chances when they'd been at the ranch. Still, he did inspire something akin to fear, she just couldn't seem to put her finger on what exactly it was.

Oh, how she wished she knew who Brook's father was, where he could be. Was he searching for them? This was one more reason for her to get to California. He had to be there, waiting for her, missing her.

Surely she'd loved him, had given herself to a man who loved her, a man who'd give his life to protect her and their child.

Maybe he'd find her, help her out of this entire mess. She closed her eyes, imagining his strong arms enfolding her, his lips whispering a promise of forever in her ear. She squeezed her eyes tightly closed against the sting of tears. Someplace out there was a man, Brook's father, Colette's prince and sooner or later they would find each other and live happily ever after. She had to believe that, she had to.

She turned away from her reflection and grabbed the jeans and blouse she'd had on before her shower. She left the bathroom, surprised to see Hank reentering the room with a duffel bag in his hand.

Sinking onto the edge of the bed, she tried to ignore how completely he seemed to fill the room. Every movement he made seethed with suppressed energy and overwhelming masculinity.

She watched as he pulled clean clothes from the duffel bag. "I don't suppose you'd have a hairbrush in there, would you?"

He frowned, as if irritated at the thought of sharing his personal items. "No brush, but I've got a comb." He pulled it from his back pocket and tossed it to her. He straightened and eyed her in speculation. "I'm going to take a shower."

She nodded, uneasy beneath the heat of his gaze. As he continued to look at her, her uneasiness increased and a flush of heat worked its way up her neck to burn her cheeks. The air seemed to thicken, vibrate with a new tension as his gaze lingered.

Her mouth grew dry and she broke the gaze, focusing instead on pulling the comb through her hair. "Hank, I told you I wouldn't try to run," she said, wondering if that's what was on his mind.

"So you said."

"You can trust me."

"Can I?" One of his dark eyebrows rose upward in a gesture of disbelief.

"Was I in the habit of breaking promises to you before I got amnesia?" she asked.

He seemed to consider her question thoughtfully. "No, I don't remember you breaking any promises."

She worked the comb through her hair, wincing as she encountered a tangle. "For heaven's sake, Hank. Go take your shower. I'm not going anywhere." She just wished he'd go, and take the uncomfortable tension with him.

"I'd feel better if I had a little insurance," he returned.

"You aren't taking Brook into the shower," Colette snapped. "She's a baby, not a bargaining chip."

"You're right. In any case, that wasn't the kind of insurance I had in mind."

"So, what?" she asked impatiently.

"Take off your pants."

Chapter Twelve

"Pardon me?" Her heart leapt into her throat.

"You heard me. Take your pants off."

"If this is some kind of a joke..."

"It's no joke, Colette. Running will be a lot less attractive to you if you're only wearing a T-shirt." He grabbed the jeans she'd been wearing before she'd showered and looked at her expectantly. "Now please, don't make me physically remove those pants from you."

"You wouldn't dare," she exclaimed, rising from the bed to face him.

He grinned, as always the gesture not quite alleviating the shadows in his eyes. "Don't tempt me." He hesitated a moment. "What are you afraid of, Colette?" His voice was as silky smooth as a snake oil salesman's.

"Nothing. Don't be ridiculous. I'm not afraid of anything," she countered.

"I'll tell you what. I'll make sure this will be the only time I'll force you to take your pants off for me."

"Oh, honestly." She quickly removed the sweatpants, grateful for the length of the T-shirt. His gaze swept the length of her bare legs, making her wish the shirt extended to the floor. Beneath the heat of his eyes she felt far too vulnerable, and the vulnerability created anger. ''There,'' she exclaimed as she threw the pants to him.

''Thank you,'' he returned evenly. ''And as I said, I won't force you to take them off again.'' A wicked smile curved his lips and his dark eyes gleamed with a heat that burned her from across the room. ''The next time you take them off for me, it will be because you want to.'' Without giving her a chance to reply, he picked up the bag of items he'd bought and disappeared into the bathroom.

Colette fought the impulse to throw something at the door, vent her frustration, the rage his arrogant self-assurance provoked. And the thing that frustrated her most was the possibility that he might be right.

She finished combing her hair, then settled back against the headboard on the bed where Brook slept. She couldn't deny that she was sexually attracted to Hank, but that certainly didn't mean she intended to follow through on the attraction.

She had to hold on to her belief that before her amnesia, before she'd overheard the dreadful conversation that had placed her in this situation, there had been a man in her life, a special man whom she'd loved. Brook's father. Whoever he was, she just knew she'd loved him to distraction and she wouldn't sully that love by indulging herself in a few moments of lust with Hank Cooper.

The sound of the running shower filled the room. She thought about turning on the television, then decided not to, preferring the relative silence to the sit-com reruns that would be on at this time of the night.

What were Abby and Belinda doing at this moment? She frowned as she imagined their horror. They'd discover quickly not only that she was missing, but also that her window had been shot out and bullet holes decorated the wall of her room.

If only she could call them, just let them know she and Brook were all right. She looked at the phone and frowned, remembering Hank had pocketed the cord.

Frustration built in her. She wouldn't have to say anything that would put her sisters at risk, wouldn't have to say anything that would put her and Hank in further danger. All she wanted to do was assure them she was okay.

On impulse she got up off the bed and approached the bathroom door. It wasn't closed all the way and steam swirled out like slender ghostly fingers. If she could just get to that cord. In a matter of seconds she could hook it back into the phone and make the call. All she needed was that damned cord.

Sucking in a deep breath, she pushed the door open an inch, grateful there was no telltale squeak. Gaining courage, she shoved it open another couple of inches and spied Hank's jeans in a pile on the floor.

Just beneath the splatter of the water against the tub, she could hear him humming. The scent of soap hung heavy in the air and the steam continued to roll out from above the plastic shower curtain.

Sinking to her hands and knees, Colette kept her gaze firmly fixed on his jeans as she crawled forward. She could see the end of the phone cord peeking out from the pocket. She couldn't see anything through the opaque curtain, so assumed he couldn't see outside the shower.

She crawled forward another couple of inches, her heart thundering as her fingers closed around the cord. Now if she could just get out of here and use the phone before he finished his shower.

Scooting back out of the bathroom, she prayed he couldn't hear the sound of her frantic heartbeat over the sound of the running water. Once outside of the bathroom, she pulled the door closed, then jumped up and raced toward the phone.

It took her a moment to plug the cord into the wall socket, then into the back of the phone. Her fingers shook as she punched in the number at the ranch.

She cried out as the phone was yanked out of her hand from behind. She whirled around to see Hank, clad only in a towel draped around his hips, his body still wet and his eyes flashing danger.

"Dammit, Colette, I thought I could trust you," he yelled. With one swift tug, he snapped the cord from the wall socket and tossed the phone across his bed.

"I just wanted to call my sisters, tell them I'm all right." Hot tears burned at her eyes.

"And I told you, it's not safe to call them."

Colette sank to her knees on the floor, suddenly overwhelmed by everything. The day's events were too much, the shooting, the chase, the total isolation from those she loved and trusted.

The tears that had stung her eyes now trekked down her cheeks unchecked. "I just wanted to hear their voices...I just...I feel so all alone."

He took her by the shoulders and pulled her to her

feet, then held her against his still damp chest. "You aren't alone. I'm here."

His words, softly spoken, combined with the strength of his arms around her back, caused sobs to erupt from deep within her. She leaned into him, needing the warmth of the human connection to battle the chill that had taken residence in her body from the moment she'd realized her memories were gone.

She mourned now the loss of those memories, cried from fear and frustration, ached with the thought that she might never remember Brook's father, might never remember love.

Coiling her arms around Hank's neck, she gave in to the sobs, letting them overtake her as she leaned weakly into his strength.

His hands rubbed up and down her back as he murmured softly, attempting to comfort her. Within minutes her sobs had ceased and she knew she should pull away from him, step out of his warm embrace. But she lingered, reluctant to leave the protective circle of his arms.

As her tears ceased, she became aware of other sensations. His skin smelled good, so clean and fresh. His chest beneath her cheek was smooth skin over hard muscle. Velvet-covered steel.

Fear subsided, her loneliness fell away as she realized how intimately they were pressed together. His bare legs against hers, nothing but his towel and her shirt separating them from each other.

His hands no longer caressed her back in an effort to comfort, but rather languidly worked up and down, evoking fire where they touched. He no longer whispered gentle, comforting words in her ear; his breathing had quickened, just as her own had.

She raised her head to look at him and gasped as she saw the fire in his eyes creating a flame that ignited deep within her.

"Colette," he murmured, then his lips claimed hers in a fiery kiss that stole her breath and banished any rational thoughts.

She tightened her arms around his neck, rising up on tiptoe to more fully experience the depth of his kiss. The silken strands of his hair curled around her fingers, beckoning her to bury her fingers in their richness.

Shivers of delight danced up her spine as his tongue deepened the kiss, touching first the edge of her teeth, then swirling deeper.

All thoughts of danger and uncertainty faded beneath the onslaught of his kiss. Fear fell away as desire swelled, banishing everything else from her mind except the pleasurable sensations soaring through her.

She gasped as his hands moved up beneath her shirt, stroking the bare skin of her back as his mouth left hers and traveled down the line of her jaw. Her gasp transformed into a moan as his hands cupped her buttocks, pulling her solidly against him, letting her know the extent of his arousal.

This is madness! her mind screamed. But her body begged for more, wanting the insanity of this passion to last forever. She was lost in his heat and wanted to remain lost until the ache that was building inside her was sated.

She frowned as she heard a noise rising above the

sound of their ragged breathing, louder than the beating of their hearts. A baby. Brook.

Brook's cry sliced through her passion-induced haze and Colette stepped away from Hank, grateful that he didn't try to hold on to her. "I'm sorry...that was foolish..." Colette's face burned.

"Probably a reaction of stress," he said, and she flashed him a grateful look.

"Yes, I'm sure that's it."

"You'd better take care of the kid."

Irritation swept through Colette, a welcomed diversion from other, more frightening emotions. "She has a name. Her name is Brook."

"Whatever." He turned and disappeared back into the bathroom.

Colette sank down next to Brook, who fussed and sputtered halfhearted cries, on the bed. She was probably wet, Colette thought. As she changed the baby's diaper, she thought of those moments in Hank's arms.

How easily he'd brought her to the brink of submission. How masterful his caresses, his kisses had been to evoke such a violent response in her.

Had Brook not cried, they would have made love. There was no doubt in Colette's mind. He would have taken her, and she would have willingly succumbed. With a few mind-numbing kisses, he'd managed to banish all thoughts of Brook's father from her mind. What kind of a woman was she? To respond so easily to a man who'd kidnapped her and intended to take her to a trial that would put the rest of her life at risk?

After changing Brook, Colette pulled down the bedspread and got into bed, confused and disturbed by her quicksilver response to Hank. She cuddled

Brook close against her. "Don't worry," she whispered to the little girl. "I won't forget that someplace out there is your daddy. We'll find him and everything will be all right."

She tensed as Hank came out of the bathroom, this time clad in a worn pair of sweatpants. Again she was struck by his physique. Why couldn't he have a pot belly and sunken chest? She turned over, presenting him her back.

HANK SHUT OFF the light, then got into the remaining bed. Through the windows, pale light seeped in around the curtains, making Colette and the baby visible as his eyes adjusted to the semidarkness.

He'd had the choice of being taken off this case. When Colette had disappeared, his boss had offered him an out, knowing that the entire situation had somehow gone beyond Hank's control.

However Hank had opted to stay on, needing not only to prove to his boss, but to himself that he was still the man for the job, still able to hold on to his objectivity. At the moment objectivity wasn't a problem. His hormones were.

Something about Colette Connor stirred him as no other woman had for a very long time. Lust. Pure and simple lust. He'd forgotten what it felt like, how difficult it was to fight.

"Hank?"

He tensed as her voice drifted across the small space that separated them. "What?"

"Before I ran away…before I got amnesia and we were stuck together, did we like each other? I mean, were we friends?"

"Friends?" He rolled the word around in his head. When had he ever had friends? Not for years. Not since he'd lost his dreams. Not since he became a man with nothing more to lose. "We got along all right. I wouldn't exactly say we were friends."

He heard the rustle of her covers as she turned over. "You said we were holed up in a hotel room. What did we do all day?"

"We watched television. We played cards. We paced and watched the clock."

She sighed. "I wish I could remember. I think everything would be much easier if I could just remember it all."

"Go to sleep, Colette. We've got a long day of travel ahead of us tomorrow." He didn't want to hear her voice whispering in the dark. It was too intimate, evoked too many memories.

"Good night, Hank."

"'Night."

The room fell silent, the only sounds the whisper of their breathing. Hank stared up at the ceiling, deep weariness sweeping through him. She made him tired. Fighting his feelings of lust, fearing all the things she might remember at any time, anticipating her trying to run again...all of it combined to exhaust him.

Sixteen more days. Then he would be forever rid of her. He'd forget the taste of her lips, the scent that so stirred him. He'd forget the sound of her laughter, the pain of her tears. He'd give her up to the court, then put her out of his life as effectively as he'd done with other witnesses a dozen times before.

"Hank?"

"What?" he snapped, wishing she'd shut up, go to sleep, and stop tossing and turning into his thoughts.

"Promise me everything is going to be all right."

Hank closed his eyes, hardening his heart against the plea in her words. "I never make promises."

There was a moment of silence. "Never?"

"Never," he answered firmly. "Now for heaven's sake, get some sleep," he finished, his tone harsh.

He knew the moment she fell asleep, heard the rhythm of her breathing change, deepen and slow. Slowly Hank began to relax. For the first time in months, things were back on track. He had Colette where she was supposed to be and he'd see his job through to the end.

Although he knew Colette needed to remember, to do what the prosecution wanted her to do, for the moment he was grateful she remembered nothing. As long as she didn't remember why she'd run before, it made his job easier.

She'd been right about one thing. In the time he'd known her, he'd never heard her break a promise. She didn't break them…and he didn't make them. And that's exactly why she'd run.

"WHAT THE HELL do you mean, you lost them?"

The cowboy winced beneath Collier's rage. "At least I got his license number. Trust me, I'll find them."

"Trust you?" Collier snorted derisively. "It's your fault I'm in this mess. You knew better than to come to the office in the first place. No. I'm through leaving this up to you. I'm sending out some of my boys. They'll get the job done."

"I'm guessing they're headed your way. They'll want to get someplace safe in San Bernardino as soon as possible to wait for the trial."

"I'll find them. I'll call in every damned marker owed to me." Collier heaved a sigh of aggravation. "Give me the damned license number. We'll find her. I don't care if we have to blow up all of Wyoming and half of California. I want that woman dead within the week."

"Understood." The cowboy hung up the phone, narrowing his eyes against the neon lights on the convenience store where he'd stopped to use the phone. Where before this had simply been just another job, it was now becoming personal. Colette Connor was making him look like a fool.

He shook out a cigarette from the pack in his pocket and lit one, his mind whirling. Not only did he intend to be the one to kill Colette Connor, but he would also see to it that Hank Cooper died with her. In fact, if done right, it would tie up loose ends and nobody would be looking for a murderer.

A smile curved his lips as he imagined the newspaper headlines: Tragic Murder/Suicide For Key Witness And Protecting Agent. Oh, yes. Collier would be proud of him. Hell, he'd probably pay a bonus if the murders could be done so no finger could ever point to him.

He took a drag on his cigarette, then flicked the butt away. Thoughtfully he scratched his cheek. He had work to do. He intended to be the one to find Colette and Hank. He wanted to be the one to kill them. In fact, although he wasn't about to tell Collier, he'd be willing to do this one for free.

Chapter Thirteen

Over the past several weeks, Colette had learned little things about herself, idiosyncrasies that amnesia had stolen momentarily. She'd discovered her abhorrence for the sight of blood, the fact that she hated green beans and now she realized how much she hated silence.

They had gotten up before dawn and left the motel. For the past hour they'd traveled at a fast clip down the highway, not a word spoken between them.

The sun peeked over the horizon, sending out shafts of light to dance amid the early morning clouds. It was going to be a beautiful day despite the fact that she was on her way to California for a trial that would probably make her a dead woman.

She sighed and shot a surreptitious glance at Hank. His attention was focused on the highway, his face devoid of all expression.

He was such an enigma, so hard on the surface, and yet she sensed a core of good in him that alleviated any fear she might have of him. He had a job to do and getting her to California was that job. She couldn't hate him for that.

Since the moment of awakening that morning, Colette had waffled back and forth in deciding what was best for her to do. If her memories came back or somehow the government managed to retrieve them, should she testify or not? Her head insisted she testify, do whatever she could to put Cameron Collier behind bars. However, the prospect of revenge from the man and his cohorts made her faint of heart.

She didn't want to spend the rest of her life looking over her shoulder for danger. There had to be a way out of this mess, but at the moment it eluded her.

She looked in the back seat, where Brook sat contented in the car seat. She moved her gaze back to Hank again, wanting something to occupy her thoughts besides her dilemma.

"How long will it take us to reach San Bernardino?" she asked, wanting to break the silence that had lingered too long for comfort.

"We'll be there by tomorrow night."

"Where are we going once we get there? Another four-star motel room?"

"No. There's a safe house there. That's where we'll stay from now until the end of your testimony."

"A safe house?"

He nodded. "A place owned by the government in a nice quiet suburb on the west side of the city. We'll be okay there."

"And then after I testify I just leave and wait for Collier's retribution?"

"There's another alternative. You could enter the witness protection plan."

Colette frowned. "But doesn't that mean I promise never to contact my friends or family again?" She shook her head. "No, that's not a viable option as far as I'm concerned." She stared out the window, where the sun had fully risen and chased away the last of the morning clouds. "As soon as I find Brook's father, everything will be all right," she said more to herself than to him.

"What do you mean by that?"

She shrugged. "Oh, I don't know. I just feel like I could face whatever testifying might bring if I knew Brook's father stood beside me, supported me and loved me."

"What makes you think if you find him, that's what he'll do?" He glanced at her, his dark brow arched upward. "Maybe he's just a coldhearted bastard."

Colette shook her head. "No, that's not possible. I could never love a coldhearted bastard."

"And what makes you think you love Brook's father?"

A blush warmed Colette's cheeks. "Well, because...because I wouldn't sleep with a man I didn't love."

Hank's eyes glittered darkly. "That wasn't the song you were singing last night."

The blush grew hotter as she remembered how close she'd come to falling into bed with him. "A gentleman wouldn't bring that up."

He laughed, the sound rusty, as if laughing wasn't something he did much. "Colette, I might be many things, but I never pretended to be a gentleman."

She looked down at her hands clasped together in her lap. "I will admit something about you attracts me. It's probably post-pregnancy hormones or something like that.''

He shook his head. "Can't be that for me because I've never been pregnant." His eyes sparkled wickedly as he gazed at her again. "And I feel the same kind of inexplicable lust where you're concerned."

The car interior suddenly seemed to shrink. The air grew thick and made it difficult to breathe. Colette lowered her window a couple of inches, although the warm outside air did little to relieve the heat that coiled inside her.

"It doesn't matter," she finally said. "I mean, just because we both feel it, doesn't mean we have to follow through on it. We're both adults."

"Hmm, of course the fact that we're both adults is a good reason for following through on the attraction. Get it out of our system. As long as we both understand the rules."

"Ah, yes, the rules of seduction, right? No promises, no commitment." She eyed him thoughtfully. "Have you always played by those rules?"

He was silent for so long she wondered if he would answer her at all. "A long time ago I didn't play by those rules," he finally said, his voice so soft she had to lean toward him to hear. "I committed, I promised, I married the woman of my dreams and on a rain-slick road a drunk driver destroyed it all."

"Oh, Hank. I'm so sorry." She touched his arm, unsurprised when he jerked away from her touch.

He shrugged. "It was a long time ago. A lifetime ago. There's a truck stop just ahead. We'll stop and get some breakfast."

Colette realized he wouldn't share any more of his

past with her, was probably irritated that he'd said as much as he had. Part of her was glad. The tragedy of his past only sharpened his appeal, and that's the last thing she needed.

Within minutes they sat at a table in the Star Truck Stop, waiting for their breakfast to be delivered. Hank sat facing the door, his gaze moving around the well-lit interior like a hawk seeking prey.

"Everything all right?" she asked.

"Fine. Just being cautious."

"Aren't you going to read the menu?" She gestured to the slick tri-fold menu in front of him.

"It's been my experience that the best thing to order in a place like this is the daily special."

She closed her menu. "I guess I'll trust you on this and do the same."

His lips curved up at the corners. "Ah, we're making progress. You're beginning to trust me."

"For the moment I have little choice but to trust you," she returned.

The waitress arrived to pour steaming coffee and take their orders. She cooed over Brook, winked flirtatiously at Hank and smiled briskly at Colette, then left their table.

As she sipped the hot coffee, Colette noticed that each time the door opened, Hank tensed, his eyes narrowed in wariness. "You think we're still in danger?" she asked.

"Collier knows we have to head toward California. Whoever he had working at the ranch will have told him we left. Collier's men will be looking for us."

"You don't have any idea who at the ranch might be working for Collier?"

Hank shook his head. "We ran a background check on the ranch hands, but it turned up nothing substantial on anyone."

"I know how we can fool them."

"How?"

"You could take me to Mexico instead of San Bernardino."

"Nice try." He smiled thinly. "I think I liked you better with your memory. At least then you were determined to testify against Collier."

"Then why did I run?"

His gaze slid away from hers. "Who knows? Maybe you got tired of me beating you in gin rummy, or maybe you got sick of fast food. I don't know why you ran. I only know you'd be a fool to do it again."

"I promised you I wouldn't try," she reminded him.

"And you never break promises."

She nodded. "And you never make them."

Their conversation halted as the waitress reappeared with their breakfast orders. Colette eyed the heaping plate in dismay. "Maybe I should have ordered from the menu. This special would feed three hungry women."

"Better eat what you can. Who knows where we'll be at lunchtime."

It was obvious Hank didn't intend to waste time on small talk. He attacked the meal as if afraid it might be his last. Colette ate as much as she could, then shoved her plate away and instead focused on her coffee.

There were so many questions she wanted to ask him, not only about her past, but about his own, as well. She'd placed her life and that of her daughter's in his hands, yet knew almost nothing about him.

"Are your parents alive, Hank?"

He looked up from his plate in surprise at the unexpected question. "My mother passed away when I was twenty-two and I don't know about my father. I never knew him. He divorced my mother when she was pregnant and she never heard from him again. Why?"

"Just curious. I suddenly realize I know nothing about you."

His eyes gazed at her darkly. "You don't need to know anything about me other than I intend to get you to San Bernardino alive." He focused back on his breakfast.

Colette swallowed a sigh and looked at the television bolted into the wall over the counter where a talk show host was interviewing runaway teens.

If only I'd stayed at the ranch. If only I hadn't wanted to see life in a big city, she thought. However, all the if-only's in the world couldn't change her position now.

She sat up straighter in the booth as the television displayed a breaking news story and a live picture of the Sleepy-Time Motel appeared. "Hank…look."

"Early this morning police were called to the scene of what they thought would be a bloody murder when gunshots were reported at this motel." The woman reporter paused to take a breath. "The desk clerk confirmed that the room had been rented by a single white male. However, when police entered, they found no body, no blood, only broken windows and dozens of bullet holes in both beds."

"Come on. We need to get back on the road," Hank said, his voice cutting through the horror that built in Colette.

Minutes later they were back in the car, eating up miles at the speed limit rate. "Hank…that was our room, wasn't it?" Colette finally said.

"I imagine it was," he agreed.

"But how…how did they find us? How did they know it was our room?"

"I don't know, Colette. All I do know is that it's important we keep moving. We won't stop anywhere tonight. We'll drive until we reach San Bernardino."

Colette wrapped her arms around herself and stared out at the blur of scenery. Had they slept later, they would all three be dead, shot while they slept in their beds. She shivered, a hard knot of anger growing in her stomach.

What kind of a monster was Cameron Collier? What lengths would he reach to keep her quiet? And how long could her and Hank's luck hold out?

As the miles passed, the anger ebbed, the horror of what might have happened passed. The motion of the car, along with the big breakfast lulled Colette. She fought against sleep, then with a sigh leaned her head against the window and gave in, allowing slumber and a world of dreams to overtake her.

HANK RELAXED the moment he knew she was asleep, knowing there would be no more probing questions about his past, no sharing of little details that ultimately encouraged intimacy. He'd made that mistake before and in the process had unconsciously encouraged her to expect things he couldn't give, anticipate a future he'd never share.

The tires sang against the hot pavement, singing his song of freedom. Once he got Colette to California, this particular job would be done. Maybe it was time he took a vacation. He'd been pushing himself hard for the past five years, ever since Rebecca's death.

Rebecca. He frowned, surprised to discover thoughts of her brought no sharp pain, no overwhelming rage, only a hollow ache of bittersweet loss.

He tried to conjure up a mental picture of her. Brown hair shot through with strands of gold. Hazel eyes that changed hues depending on what colors she wore. He tightened his grip on the steering wheel. Ire swept through him as he realized it wasn't Rebecca whose image unfolded in his mind, but rather Colette's.

He shot a sideways glance at her. Although she was still asleep, it was not a restful slumber. Her forehead was wrinkled and she winced, as if suffering an unpleasant dream.

It was easy to imagine the nightmares that haunted her. She was not in an enviable position. Testifying against a man like Collier was probably the most dangerous thing she'd ever do in her life. Unfortunately, at this point in time, not testifying was just as dangerous. The moment Collier learned that she'd heard the incriminating conversation between him and his hit man, Colette's head had gained a bounty.

Hopefully he could keep her safe until the trial. The prosecution would keep her safe during the trial and after that…after that she wasn't his concern. He frowned, surprised at the bitter taste in his mouth this thought produced.

He thought of her hope in finding the baby's father...the idea that somehow the father was a prince among men who'd keep her and the child safe, protect them and love them forever. She carried the dreams of an innocence he'd long ago lost. Eventually those dreams of hers would shatter beneath the weight of cold reality, but he wouldn't be around to watch it happen.

Looking in his rearview mirror, he tensed as he spotted a patrol car gaining on him. He gazed down at his speedometer and relaxed somewhat. He wasn't speeding so there should be no problem. Still as the patrol car continued to gain and the red light on the top began to spin, a bad feeling swept over Hank. Maybe he had been speeding a little. He hit the steering wheel with the palm of his hand. Just what he needed, a damned ticket.

"Colette, wake up," he said as he slowed and looked for a place to pull over onto the shoulder of the highway.

She awoke immediately. "Wha-what's wrong?"

"We have company."

She turned backward and looked behind them, where the police car rode Hank's bumper. She looked back at Hank. "Were you speeding?"

"No. At least I didn't think so." He pulled to a stop on the shoulder, the police car just behind.

Several cars whizzed by them before the officer got out of his car and approached Hank's window. The bad feeling inside Hank escalated. "Afternoon, Officer,'' he greeted the tall, pock-faced man who leaned down and peered into the car. "What's the problem?"

"I need your license and registration,'' the officer replied.

"I'll like to know why I was stopped,'' Hank replied. Every instinct he owned cried out that something was amiss.

"Routine check. Your license?''

Hank pulled his wallet from his back pocket, removed his driver's license and handed it to the officer. Routine check? Usually a routine checkpoint was set up with more officers than a single one.

"Just sit tight. I need to call this in, then you and Ms. Connor can be on your way.'' The officer stepped back to his car.

"Hang on,'' Hank muttered to Colette. "We're in trouble.'' His gaze didn't leave the rearview mirror. He was grateful she didn't say anything, didn't ask questions and scatter his concentration.

The officer sat in his car as several more vehicles went by in both directions. As the highway stretched empty of traffic once again, he got out and once again approached Hank's car.

As he reached the back fender, Hank saw his right hand move toward his gun. Hank shoved the car into gear and pulled away, his tires spewing gravel and dust before gripping the hot pavement and shooting forward.

Colette gasped and gripped her seat as he accelerated. Hank knew he had two things going for him, the element of surprise to gain him a head start, and enough horsepower under the hood to keep whatever lead he'd managed to gain.

He took the first turn he came to, getting off the highway and onto a county road. From there he made a series of turns until they found themselves on a dirt road in the middle of nowhere.

Slowing his speed, he allowed himself to take a deep breath and relax momentarily. There was no sign they had been followed and he suspected he'd managed to lose the patrolman.

"Why did you do that?" Colette finally spoke.

"Because if I hadn't, somebody would have found our dead bodies along the road." He pulled off the side of the road into a grove of trees and brush. He needed to take a moment to allow his adrenaline to die down. He shut off the engine and turned to Colette, whose eyes were wide with fear. "That cop was one of Collier's men."

"How do you know?"

"I felt it in my gut. Besides, he had no reason to stop us, and he called you Ms. Connor. There was no way he should have known your name." He opened his car door. "I need to walk a little bit."

She shot a glance into the back seat where Brook slept, then opened her car door. "Mind if I join you?"

He shook his head. Together they got out of the car. The afternoon heat shimmered, but beneath the foliage where the car was parked, the air was cooler, not unpleasant. He sat on the car hood, needing to think, to plan where they went from here.

Colette scooted up next to him, her fear almost palpable. "How did he find us? How did he know to stop us?"

"Collier must have my license plate number. He must be calling in markers all over the U.S."

She leaned against him. "What are we going to do, Hank? We can't hide from every policeman along the way."

"It's not every cop we have to worry about, just those dirty ones trying to do Collier's work."

"How do we tell the difference between the two?"

He sighed. "That's what I'm trying to figure out." He was having problems concentrating with the warmth of her body against his, the scent of her perfume filling the air.

"What we need to do is ditch the car, get on a bus or a plane or something."

"You're right." He raked a hand through his hair and frowned thoughtfully. "There's a map in the glove box. Would you get it for me?"

She nodded and slid off the hood, taking with her the scent that muddied his thoughts, made it tough to concentrate.

He stood and stretched with arms overhead, the adrenaline not dissipating, but rather building inside him. As Colette rejoined him, he took the map from her and spread it out across the hood. Peering at it, he tried to figure out exactly where they were. He knew about where they'd been when the patrol car pulled them over. "We're about here," he said, placing his index finger on the spot on the map.

Colette once again leaned against him as she looked at where he pointed. "We aren't too far from Provo."

He nodded. "It looks like we can take back roads into the city, then probably our best bet is to do as you suggested. Ditch the car and get on a plane to

San Bernardino. As long as we're in the car we're sitting ducks.''

She shivered, her eyes once again huge as she looked up at him. ''Is this what my life is going to be like from now on? Running? Hiding? I'm supposed to keep Brook safe…how can I do that when I can't even keep myself safe? If I can't trust the police, who can I trust?''

Despite his reservations, Hank pulled her into his arms, knowing she needed the physical contact of comfort to chase away the haunting fear in her eyes. Willingly she went into his embrace, molding herself to him, as if needing to crawl inside him, meld to his strength.

''Colette, for every one dirty cop, there's a thousand good ones,'' he murmured, the adrenaline pumping through him as her warmth mingled with his, her scent invaded his head.

She nodded, her hands clutching him tighter around the neck as her body burrowed closer against his. He knew he should disentangle himself from her, knew she was experiencing a common emotional response to danger. But he understood this in some distant part of his mind, a part he didn't have the willpower to tap in to. Instead he held her tight, as if absorbing her into his very pores.

All his senses seemed heightened. A bird chirped merrily overhead and a warm breeze rustled through the branches of the tree. The sounds of nature mingled with Colette's soft breaths against his neck, the noise of his own heartbeat surging within his chest.

When she looked up at him, her eyes were darkened with desire, and her gaze lit the flames of desire in him. Groaning deeply, he captured her lips with his, drinking in the sweet passion she offered.

He knew they were both functioning on sheer emotion with no thought to what was right or wrong, but he had no desire to control or change the situation. Although he knew he'd probably regret it later, at the moment he simply wanted to take whatever she offered.

She broke the kiss and took one of his hands in hers. With her eyes blazing in unspoken want, she led him to a shady, grassy area beneath the tree. She knelt down and with one smooth movement pulled her T-shirt over her head. "Hank." Her voice was as soft as a sigh, as compelling as the sunshine to a flower. "Hank, make love to me." She sank back in the grass and opened her arms toward him.

His desire for her ached through him, impossible to ignore. He could no more avoid going to her than he could bypass the act of breathing. He eased down next to her, vaguely aware of the lush coolness of the grass, but more captivated by the way she looked.

Dappled sunlight kissed her flushed skin and highlighted her wispy bra. With her chestnut-colored hair and her eyes picking up the green hues surrounding them, she looked like a woodland nymph.

He took her in his arms, his lips once again seeking hers as his hands caressed the silky smoothness of her shoulders, her back. She didn't merely accept his caresses, but rather was an active participant, her hands moving up beneath his T-shirt with featherlight touches that inflamed his senses.

I should stop this, he thought as his fingers fumbled with the clasp on her bra. *One of us has to be strong.*

This is crazy. But these thoughts were lost as her bra fell away, exposing her full breasts to his heated gaze, his reverent touch.

With his last vestige of control he knew he had to make her understand that there was no forever for them, nothing but this moment of need, this space of time here and now. He had nothing to offer her.

"Colette," he murmured against the hollow of her neck. "Colette, you have to understand…"

"I know, your rules of seduction. No promises, no commitments." Her voice was breathy, husky with desire. "Don't worry, I promise I won't forget the rules. Just love me, Hank."

Her words snapped the last strand of his control. He sat back only long enough to pull his shirt over his head, then rejoined her in the sweet grass.

COLETTE REVELED in the passion that had been building between them since the moment she'd first seen him at the ranch. His kisses filled her soul, his caresses burned her flesh and she wanted him with a ferocity that overwhelmed her.

Each touch from him spawned renewed fire inside her, every caress carried her higher and higher. And somewhere in the back of her mind was the same strange familiarity, as if they'd been lovers in another lifetime. It was haunting, disturbing, but the impression fled as he removed her sweatpants, his hot hands stroking each inch of flesh as he bared it.

She unbuckled his belt, her fingers trembling with want, with need. He'd used the same belt to hold her captive only the night before, but now she was a willing captive, his prisoner by her own design.

With her help, he removed his jeans and within moments they were both naked. Her hands danced across the muscles and planes of his body, caressing and exploring as he did the same to her.

Their rapid breathing filled the air, mingling with husky moans and gasps of pleasure. The residual of fear, of danger that had been with her for so long, faded beneath the onslaught of passion each of Hank's caresses evoked.

When he finally entered her, Colette's heart swelled and tears sprang to her eyes. They were tears of joy. He filled every empty space she'd held in her heart, in her soul. It was the only thing that had felt right in her life since she'd lost her memories.

He moved deeply, slowly within her, taking her higher and higher, leading her to the edge of a precipice. As she went over the edge, she grasped his back and cried out, her cries carrying him with her.

For a long moment neither of them moved, but rather remained locked in their embrace. Colette could feel his heart beating against her own, the rhythms matching as they began to slow to a more normal beat.

With the satiation of passion came the return of reality. As breathtaking as this interlude had been, nothing had changed. Hank was still taking her to a trial, men still intended to try to kill her and they were stuck in the middle of nowhere with a car whose license tags were like a neon invitation to all of Collier's men.

They dressed silently, the earlier intimacy replaced by an awkward silence. "We'd better get moving," he finally said.

She nodded, vaguely disappointed to see the cold distance in his eyes. Okay, so that's the way it's going to be, she thought as she walked back to the car. They would pretend they hadn't just made love. After all, she'd promised no commitments, no hope for anything other than that single moment in time. They'd satiated their lust, alleviated inner tension, nothing more.

It was back to the cold of reality. They had to get to San Bernardino. She had to find Brook's father... before Collier's men found them.

Chapter Fourteen

It took them an hour to get to Provo, using back roads and dirt trails to finally make it into the city. Once there, they parked the car in a shopping mall garage and sought a pay phone. Hank called the airport, dismayed to discover the earliest flight to San Bernardino was eight hours away.

"I don't want to hang around for eight hours," he said with a frown as he hung up the phone.

"Maybe we can catch a bus right away," Colette suggested. "Besides, I'm not real thrilled about flying."

Hank leaned against the phone stand and rubbed his forehead thoughtfully. "The bus is probably better anyway. The first thing they'll do if and when they find the car is guess that we got on a plane."

She nodded absently. "Hank...please let me call my sisters." She eyed the phone longingly, then looked back at him. "I need to let them know I'm safe." She didn't know how he would respond to her plea. He'd been emotionally removed from her since the moment they'd finished making love and gotten back into the car. "Hank, it's important to me."

"Colette, it's just not smart."

"I don't care whether it's smart or not. I want to call and I'm not moving a foot from this phone until I do." She raised her chin defiantly.

"Colette, be reasonable." A muscle ticked in Hank's jaw, an open display of irritation.

"I'm tired of being reasonable. I know Abby and Belinda must be frantic. I've promised you I wouldn't try to run again. I'm committed to seeing this whole mess through, but I'm serious about this. If you don't let me make this call, you'll have to carry me kicking and screaming away from here."

He hesitated a moment, the jaw muscle working overtime; he dug out a handful of change and handed it to her. As she deposited the money and dialed, he walked several steps away from the phone to give her some semblance of privacy.

Abby answered and the sound of her voice immediately brought thick emotion to Colette's throat. "Abby?" She swallowed against her tears as Abby responded half hysterically. It took her a few moments to calm Abby, reassure her that everything was fine and Colette and Brook safe.

"But where are you?" Abby asked when Colette had explained the situation to her.

"I can't say, but we're on our way to San Bernardino. We should be there sometime tomorrow."

"Then what?" Abby asked.

"Hank says we'll stay in a safe house, a place in a quiet little suburb where nobody will find us. We'll stay there until the trial...then I don't know what will happen."

"I do. You'll come home," Abby answered in her no-nonsense tone.

"But, Abby, if Collier goes to prison, that doesn't mean he won't try to get revenge on me."

"I don't give a damn if he sends an army after you, you belong here at the ranch with us."

Colette closed her eyes and gripped the phone closer against her ear, grateful for the love and support that radiated to her over the line. "Before I come home I want to try to find Brook's father. I need to know why he's not with me, what's kept him from me. I need to know if he's my prince."

Abby didn't answer for a moment, and Colette wondered if Abby was thinking of the three little girls they had been, each hoping for a prince to marry them and be their soul mates for life. "Do what you need to do Colette, but know Belinda and I are here for you no matter what happens."

"I know. Somehow I'll stay in touch," Colette replied, then, saying goodbye, she hung up. She turned to Hank, who stood some distance away with his back to her. She shifted Brook from one arm to the other, sorry they'd left the car seat behind. "Thank you," she said softly as she touched his arm.

He spun around, the aloofness still on his features, in the dispassionate way he glanced at her. "Let's get going."

The bus station was nearly a mile away from where they'd left the car. Colette shifted the baby from arm to arm, trying to keep up with Hank's long strides and fighting down a wave of irritation.

From the moment she'd tapped into his passion, he'd turned off his emotions. After the explosive lovemaking they'd shared, how could he be so detached? So cool and unapproachable?

Or was it fear? She toyed with this thought, wondering if perhaps he was afraid that because they made love, she'd expect something more from him. Maybe he was afraid she'd demand an emotional commitment, she'd desire a surrogate father for Brook if she couldn't find the real thing.

Had his wife's death scarred him so deeply that he feared any commitment of any kind to another woman? She thought of Abby. She'd given her heart to a cowboy who'd abandoned her and now swore she'd never give love a second chance. Deep love apparently caused devastating scars.

She wondered if she'd loved Brook's father that deeply and would her heart grow a hard shell if she discovered Brook's father was an uncaring man who wanted nothing to do with either his child or her mother? Somehow Colette couldn't see herself losing faith in love, no longer believing in a happily-ever-after ending for herself and her daughter.

All she had to do to get to her happy ending was avoid an army of hitmen, testify in the trial of a powerful killer and find the man she loved despite the fact she couldn't remember a thing about him. A wave of hopelessness swept through her and she moved closer to Hank, somehow feeling safer even walking in his shadow.

The bus station was a squat building that appeared to waver in the afternoon heat. Once inside, Hank bought two tickets, obviously pleased that the next bus left within the hour. "We'd better grab a hot dog or something," he said, pointing to a concession.

"Who knows how often the bus will stop between here and our destination."

Moments later they sat at one of the small tables surrounding the concession stand, hot dogs and sodas in front of them. "This tastes wonderful," Colette said.

Hank smiled, the first gesture of warmth since their lovemaking. "You're a cheap date if you can be satisfied with a hot dog."

"It depends on how much time has passed between meals," she replied, warmed by his smile and the crack in his seeming indifference. "It seems like it's been a long time since breakfast. I'm hungry enough that you probably could have bought me a pretzel and I'd have been happy."

As usual, his gaze didn't stay on her, but rather swept the perimeters of their area, always watchful, always wary, reminding Colette that they were a long way from her happy ending.

"Is everything all right?" she asked.

He nodded. "As far as I can tell. Until they find the car, they'll be searching the highways looking for us. I think, at least for the moment, we can relax."

"I won't relax fully until this is all over, and even then, from what you've told me, I'll probably never be able to completely relax ever again." She stroked Brook's head and smiled as the baby gurgled in contentment. She looked back at Hank. "I will testify. If somebody can make my memories return, I'll testify and face whatever the consequences."

"I thought you weren't sure about it, that you would rather run or face charges than face Collier's revenge. What changed your mind?'' He studied her curiously.

She sat back in the seat, frowning thoughtfully. ''I'm not exactly sure what changed my mind. I think it was when you told me that policeman was one of Collier's thugs and probably intended to kill us.'' She hugged Brook tighter. ''He probably would have killed Brook, too.''

''Probably,'' Hank agreed, his voice low.

''A man capable of ordering something like that, men capable of doing things like that, need to be stopped, no matter how high the price. I have to testify, it's the right thing to do.'' She crumpled up the paper that had wrapped her hot dog. ''Besides, logically I know whether I testify or not, Collier isn't the kind of man to be talked out of revenge. As long as I'm alive, I'm at risk. At least with him behind bars, the risk lessens somewhat.''

''That's the way you felt before. You were determined, despite the danger involved, to testify, to do everything in your power to put Collier away.'' His gaze captured hers, dark and enigmatic, yet causing a stir of heat deep inside her. ''For what it's worth, I admire your courage.''

''It's worth a lot,'' she answered, looking down to escape the intensity of his gaze. When he looked at her that way, his eyes like bottomless pits of flames, her skin tingled with the feel of his caresses and an ache grew inside her, the ache to have him hold her, kiss her, love her again.

It bothered her how much his opinion of her mattered. She shouldn't care what he thought of her. After all, in a matter of days, once the trial began, she'd probably never see him again.

"We'd better get to our gate," he said as he stood and picked up his duffel bag. "We should be loading soon."

Once again she sensed his emotional distance, his gaze no longer heated but rather remote and wary as he scanned the small group that shared the terminal with them.

His wariness continued as they boarded the bus and he eyed each person who got on. Each and every person underwent complete scrutiny as they found their seats and settled in for the long ride.

Hank didn't relax until the bus was loaded and on its way, then he leaned back in his seat and breathed an audible sigh. Colette felt a mirroring release of tension. She leaned back in the seat and closed her eyes.

It was difficult to believe so much had happened in the space of two days. She'd been shot at, kidnapped, tied up, and made love to...an emotional roller-coaster ride that had left her momentarily drained.

She shifted in her seat and looked out at the passing scenery, grateful Hank had chosen to sit on the aisle, leaving her the window seat. She was not grateful that the seats were too close, too small to accommodate two people and a baby without inadvertent touch. Hank's thigh pressed against hers and their arms grazed each other as they shared the arm rest between them.

His scent surrounded her and she wasn't sure

whether it emanated from him or lingered on her own skin from their earlier lovemaking.

Brook gave a lusty cry, one Colette immediately identified as probably hunger. "Could you hand me her bottle from your duffel bag?" Colette asked Hank.

He nodded curtly and handed her the bottle. Colette fed her daughter, grateful to concentrate on anything other than Hank and making love to him.

It wasn't really making love, she reminded herself. Rather it had been an explosion of tension, a release, a momentary escape from the madness and fear into the arms of strength and togetherness. The threat of death had ignited an enormous hunger for life. But it hadn't been love that had brought them together.

It troubled her that no matter what they'd shared, no matter what it was called in her head, she wanted it again. She wanted to be in his arms once more, feeling him move inside her, filling up the emptiness inside her.

Fifteen more days, then the trial would begin and Hank would be out of her life forever. She'd be free to find Brook's father, seek her happily-ever-after. This thought should have brought with it relief, but instead she only felt a dull depression settling over her shoulders.

FIFTEEN MORE DAYS. The count of days when he'd finally be rid of Colette was becoming a mantra of sorts. Hank hadn't considered how difficult the bus ride would be, how close their quarters would be for the duration of the ride.

They'd spent the first two hours of the trip in silence, Colette whispering softly to the baby and Hank trying to ignore them both. Realizing it was impossible to ignore them, for the past several hours he and Colette had indulged in the kind of small talk Hank usually abhorred.

They speculated on the other passengers, making up stories about their life-styles and occupations. Colette did most of the talking, while Hank listened, half amused, half irritated by her imaginative flair. Her stories amused him, but it irritated him how much he enjoyed watching her features as she spun her tales.

He was grateful when night fell and he could no longer see the sparkle of her eyes, the sensual shape of her lips. He only wished the darkness would mute the scent of her, the feel of her body heat radiating toward him, as well.

Leaning his head against the seat, he closed his eyes. The shooting at the motel bothered him, the fact that somebody had gotten that close, missing them only by mere minutes. Had he slept fifteen minutes longer, had Colette taken a little more time in getting dressed, their blood would have been splattered all over the walls of the room.

At least for the moment they were safe. Ditching the car had been a good idea and had probably bought them some time. Hopefully by the time Collier's men found the car, he and Colette would already be at the safe house.

He hadn't truly relaxed for months. Now, knowing they were safe for the moment, he felt the last of his tension ebb from him.

He jerked awake, surprised that he'd been able to sleep at all. Looking at his watch, he realized he'd been asleep for a little over two hours. The bus was quiet except the occasional cough or throat-clearing of another passenger and the hum of the engine as it carried them along.

He looked over at Colette. Her head rested against the window and she appeared to be asleep, but it wasn't the kind of deep, refreshing sleep he'd just enjoyed.

She moved restlessly, shifting the baby from arm to arm as a frown etched a wrinkle across her forehead. A stab of empathy swept through him. He wondered if her frown came from the content of her dreams, or from the physical discomfort of wrestling the baby for the last several hours.

He couldn't help change her dreams, but he could do something to relieve the burden of the baby. Before he'd thought it through, before giving himself an opportunity to change his mind, he reached for the child.

Colette's eyes flew open, panicked as her hold tightened. "It's all right," he said softly. "I'll hold her for a while so you can sleep better."

She smiled, her gaze soft as she relinquished the sleeping baby to his arms. "Thanks, my arms are so tired." Her eyes remained a soft hue of spring grass mixed with a hint of summer sky. "You're a nice man, Hank," she murmured, then closed her eyes and within seconds was sound asleep.

Hank wanted to jostle her awake, tell her he was not a nice man. He was a heartless bastard and she'd do well to remember that.

Already he regretted his offer to hold the baby. As she wiggled against his chest, seeking comfort against the unaccustomed angles, her powder-sweet scent surrounded him.

Hank closed his eyes, seeking the impenetrable shell that protected his heart, his sanity. Brook snuggled against him as if certain of her welcome, her fingers closing around Hank's thumb.

Long ago this had been Hank's dreams, his hopes. A wife, a child, the kind of family he'd never had when growing up. Rebecca had carried the seeds of his dreams when she'd been killed. The drunk had gone to jail on two counts of vehicular manslaughter, one for Rebecca and another for the unborn child she'd carried. He should have had a third charge against him, for on that rain-slick night, a vital part of Hank had died, as well.

Colette had managed to stir the flames of his passion, something he'd never thought would happen again, but she would be crazy to try to breathe new life into his heart. He'd stopped caring five years ago, and nothing and nobody could jump-start a heart irrevocably broken.

He opened his eyes as the baby shifted positions and started to cry. "Shh." He patted her little back, wondering if she, too, suffered bad dreams like her mother.

"She's probably hungry. Give her a bottle and she'll go back to sleep," Colette muttered, still half asleep.

Hank reached into the duffel bag and withdrew the bottle, then rearranged the baby so he could feed her. As she sucked on the nipple, she stared up at him.

Not blinking, not wavering, her gaze seemed to peer through to his very soul. And even though he knew he was being silly, even though he knew she was just a baby, nothing more, he felt as if he saw judgment in her dark eyes. With the eyes of an innocent, the eyes of truth, she'd found him a coward.

Fifteen more days, he told himself. Fifteen more days and this would all be behind him. Colette and Brook would be out of his life forever.

"SHE CALLED THE RANCH." The cowboy waited for Collier's reaction, proud that he'd decided to sit tight at the ranch, knowing Colette would let her sisters know where she was at the first opportunity.

"And?" Collier said impatiently.

"And she told her sister she's being taken to a safe house in San Bernardino."

Collier laughed, the cold sound rippling the skin on the nape of the cowboy's neck. "Good, good. I've got a man on the inside of the police department. He'll be able to get me the address of this 'safe' house. Finally I see the end of this untimely inconvenience."

"Mr. C. When you get the address, give it to me. Let me be the one to take care of this."

"And why should I do that? You've managed to screw this up a number of times. I won't go to prison and right now Colette is the only person who can put me there. This matter should have been disposed of months ago. I can't afford another screw-up."

"I know, I know."

"Then I repeat, why should I give it to you?"

The cowboy gripped the phone receiver more tightly. "Because I want her dead as much, if not more, than you do."

Again Collier laughed. ''Okay, call me in an hour and I'll have the address, but I'm warning you...if you blow it this time, I'll personally put a bullet in the center of your forehead.''

Chapter Fifteen

Dawn brought with it a renewed conviction in Colette, the knowledge that she'd made the right choice in deciding to testify no matter what the consequences. Splashes of gorgeous colors lit the eastern sky, filling her with an optimism she hadn't felt for months.

Within hours they would be at the safe house. Safe. She couldn't remember the last time she'd felt truly safe. She frowned, realizing that wasn't exactly true.

She could remember the last time. She'd felt safe while in the circle of Hank's arms. She looked over to him, her heart expanding as she stared at the picture he made with her daughter sleeping soundly on his chest.

The pale predawn light softened the harshness of his features. Forbidding when awake, slumber brought a more subdued strength coupled with a relaxed softness that touched Colette in her heart.

At that moment Colette knew she'd done the unthinkable. She'd broken her promise to him. She didn't understand his rules of seduction at all. She'd somehow managed to fall in love with him.

Leaning her head against the seat, she closed her eyes and swallowed a moan. How could this have happened? How on earth in the space of two days had she managed to lose her heart to Hank Cooper?

She frowned. Had it happened in two days? Or had the seeds of love been planted before she'd lost her memories, in those days she and Hank had shared while in hiding?

He'd told her they'd basically been strangers, forced into pseudo-intimacy because of their positions. Yet, when she'd made love with him, she'd felt the stirrings of familiarity, as if they'd been lovers many times before.

She looked at him again. Lover or liar? And if he was lying about their past relationship…why?

She suddenly found herself staring into the dark depths of his eyes. "You're staring," he said.

"Yes…I…" She flushed, grateful he couldn't read her mind. "I'll take Brook now. You held her nearly all night." She took the baby from him and cuddled her sleepy warmth close.

She stared out the window, confused by her thoughts. She didn't want to be in love with Hank. He was nothing like her idea of the prince she'd dreamed of as a young girl.

She wanted to be in love with Brook's father, whoever he was, wherever he was. She needed to believe that Brook had been conceived from the fire of a forever kind of love, not the temporary spark of a one-night stand or a lust connection.

Hank had made it very clear from his rules of seduction that he wasn't looking for any kind of a relationship. He'd made it perfectly clear he was a loner and intended to stay that way. He wouldn't want a wife, to raise another man's daughter. He certainly wasn't a forever kind of man.

Perhaps she was just fooling herself and pretending to love Hank, she thought. After all, at the moment he was the only stable, safe harbor. Probably her feelings for him were natural under the circumstances. With this thought in mind, she relaxed somewhat, hoping it was just a matter of time before she found Brook's father, found her one true love.

The morning hours passed slowly. Twice the bus stopped for gas, allowing the passengers to grab something to eat and stretch their legs before continuing the journey.

With each hour that brought them closer to San Bernardino, Hank seemed to grow more distant and more tense. Brook grew fussy, as if subtly picking up Hank's tension.

By the time they pulled into the San Bernardino bus station, a stirring of responding crankiness raked through Colette. Her body ached from the hours cramped in the seat, her arms were exhausted from wrestling Brook. She was irritated by Hank's withdrawal and anxious from his wariness.

"I'll make a quick phone call, then we'll rent a car to get to the safe house," he said once they'd left the bus.

Colette nodded and followed him to a pay phone. He deposited a quarter then punched in a series of numbers. "Yeah, it's me," he said into the receiver. "We're here and on our way to grandmother's house." He listened a moment or two, then uttered a goodbye and hung up.

"'Grandmother's house'?'' Colette repeated as they walked toward the rental car counter.

"The safe house used to belong to one of our agent's grandmother. Since the government bought it, we've always referred to it as grandmother's house."

Their conversation ceased as he went about the business of renting the car. Once they were settled in a midsize sedan, Colette attempted conversation again.

"So how far is it to grandmother's house?" she asked, patting Brook's back as the little girl fussed wearily.

"About fifteen minutes from here." He eyed the baby and frowned. "Is the kid all right?"

"Her name is Brook," Colette snapped. "Why do you have a problem calling her that? And no, she's not all right. She's tired of being held and cranky because her schedule is all topsy-turvy." She sighed. "I guess I'm just a little cranky, too."

"Cranky is allowed after a long bus ride." He offered her a tired half smile. "Once we get to the house we can relax and you can get Brook back on some sort of schedule."

"How did you get chosen for this particular assignment anyway?" she asked.

"This is what I do…what I've done for the past ten years. I guard witnesses, keep them safe until they testify in court against people who don't want them to speak."

"Have you guarded lots of women, or am I your first?" She blushed at the sexual connotation in the latter of her question.

His half grin widened. "No, you aren't my first. There have been several women over the years."

She gazed out the window, wondering if those women had tasted his lips, felt his body move against theirs, his moans whisper in their ears. Not that she cared. She'd decided whatever she felt for Hank couldn't be love. She was in love with Brook's father. What she felt for Hank was some sort of attraction magnified by their forced closeness.

"I thought you said we were only fifteen minutes from the house," she said a few minutes later. "I get the feeling we're driving around in circles."

"We are," he agreed. "Just making sure we aren't being followed."

"The first thing I intend to do is take a long, hot shower."

"Hmm, and I want a big meal, anything that doesn't come wrapped in cellophane or biodegradable paper."

"Will there be food there or will we have to grocery shop?"

"The house is fully furnished and the pantries should be completely stocked. You won't be sticking your head out the door for anything until the prosecutor sends a car to pick you up for the trial."

"I'm going to need some more things for Brook."

He nodded. "Whatever you need, let me know and I'll get it for you."

"We should be fine until tomorrow, then I'll need some more formula and diapers." It was easier to focus on these mundane things in an effort to ignore the electricity that sizzled in the air between them.

It was the same electricity that had been building

from the moment they had finished making love. Their lovemaking had only provided a temporary respite and she knew the charged air was desire building again, needing to be sated once more.

Colette didn't intend to let it happen again. The first time had confused her enough. She needed to keep some distance from Hank, knew it would be far too easy to allow the circumstances of their forced closeness to dictate her heart.

"This is it," he said as he finally pulled into the driveway of a small, nondescript house in a quiet neighborhood.

This was where she'd spend the next fourteen days of her life, Colette thought as she looked at the house with interest. Painted white, with Wedgwood blue shutters, the house and lawn looked well kept, as if owned by a family with pride. "It looks nice." It certainly didn't look like a government-owned place for keeping witnesses.

"Come on, let's get inside and get you that shower and I'll see if I can rustle us up something to eat."

Inside, the house welcomed with comfortable furniture in earth tones and the lingering scent of lemon oil. "At least it's clean," Hank said as he set his duffel bag down. "The last time I came here it looked like a pigpen. I raised all kinds of hell."

"Your hellraising must have worked. It looks spotless." She walked through the living room and peeked into the kitchen, where the countertops gleamed and the kitchen table sported a centerpiece of wooden fruit.

From the kitchen she went down a short hallway, stopping at the first doorway that led to a bedroom.

A double bed, dresser drawers and a nightstand gave the room a functional air. The floral bedspread and matching curtains added a touch of warmth.

The second bedroom held a double bed, but also had a crib shoved into one corner. "They knew you'd be bringing Brook," Hank said from behind her.

He stood so close to her she felt his breath on the nape of her neck. She moved farther into the room, away from him. "Looks like I'll bunk in here." She placed Brook on the bed and turned to look at Hank. "If you'll bring me Brook's things from your duffel bag, I think I'll give her a quick sponge bath and put her down in the crib. She'll probably be happy to sleep without being held for a change."

His gaze shot from the bed, back to her, and for a moment she saw a flame light his eyes, a flame that beckoned her. Her mouth grew dry as she realized he was thinking of her on the bed with him. "Hank...Brook's things?" she said, needing to break the spell.

"Yeah, right." He turned, left, and was back a moment later with the baby items he'd carried in his duffel bag. He tossed them onto the bed, then left the room without another word.

Colette drew in a deep breath, her fingers shaking slightly as she undressed Brook. How was she ever going to spend the next fourteen days with Hank in this house and not fall into the fire of his eyes?

Carrying Brook into the bathroom, Colette tried to shove thoughts of Hank away. She found a washcloth beneath the sink and focused her attention on giving Brook a bath. She laughed as the little girl squirmed and waved her arms in the air, obviously enjoying the feel of the warm cloth against her naked skin.

Once Brook was clean, rediapered and in a fresh sleeper, Colette gave her a bottle, then put her down for a nap. She stood for a long moment by the side of the crib, loving her daughter, wondering if they had a future.

"Colette?" Hank appeared in her doorway. "I've got a couple of steaks ready to eat."

She followed him into the kitchen. He'd set the table and on each plate was a large steak and a baked potato. "How'd you manage this in such a short time?" she asked in amazement as she slid into a chair at the table.

"The miracles of modern technology." He pointed to a microwave on the countertop. "Broiled steaks and zapped potatoes only take minutes." He scooted into the chair across from her.

They fell on the food like hungry vultures; no need for conversation as they fed the more basic need of hunger. The only sounds in the room were the clinking of their silverware and the steady tick-tock of a big-faced clock above the stove.

As Colette finished the meal, she became more aware of the ticking of the clock, the passing of time. She wanted time to pass fast, to carry her quickly to trial and on with the rest of her life. This place and Hank were interims from life, a kind of limbo that could possibly become a blend of heaven and hell.

"Hank, what happens if I don't get back my memories?"

He shoved his plate aside and looked at her thoughtfully. "I'm not sure. It will be up to the prosecutors how to handle it.'' He stood and carried his plate to the sink. ''But we're still fourteen days out from the trial. A lot of things can happen in fourteen days.''

''Don't remind me,'' Colette returned, also rising and picking up her plate. ''You cooked, I'll do cleanup.''

''I'll help. There isn't much else to do.''

As she filled the sink with soapy water, he carried the last of the dishes on the table to her. ''I asked you this before, but it was at a time when you weren't telling me much, where are you from, Hank? Where's home?''

''I think I told you then, here and there. That was pretty much the truth.'' He picked up a dishtowel to dry the dishes as she washed and rinsed them. ''I rent a room not far from here, but I don't spend much time there.''

''How did you learn so much about horses? You looked like a natural at the ranch.''

''My mother was a horsewoman, raised and bred them on a ranch in North Carolina. I think I learned to ride before I could walk.'' He wiped a plate and replaced it in the cabinet, then leaned against the counter. ''I will tell you this, being at your ranch made me remember how much I once loved that kind of life.'' He picked up another plate. ''Who knows, perhaps when this case is finished, I'll find myself a ranch and go back to breaking horses.''

''You could always come back to our place.'' The words flew out of Colette's mouth without forethought. She forced a laugh. ''I might be in need of a horse-breaking bodyguard when this is all over.''

He eyed her darkly, his sensual lips upturned in a smile that threatened to steal Colette's breath away. "I'm probably not the best candidate for guarding your body. In fact, I'm afraid I have to admit that at the moment I'm thinking thoughts that have nothing to do with guard duty."

Colette tore her gaze from his, refusing to fall into the sensual web his dark eyes spun. "I think I hear Brook crying." She dried her hands and escaped the kitchen and Hank's heated gaze.

HANK KNEW Brook hadn't cried, knew in truth Colette had run from the desire he'd been fighting since the moment they'd finished making love yesterday. He finished the dishes, then threw himself onto the sofa in the living room, trying not to think of the taste of her, the feel of her.

Outside evening shadows encroached on the last of the day's light, shrouding the room in purple twilight. He flipped on the light on the end table, vaguely aware of the sound of the water running in the bathroom. Colette must be having her long-awaited shower.

He frowned, an image of her standing beneath the spray teasing his mind. Somehow, someway she'd managed to crawl under his skin. He wanted her with a mindless intensity, a craving that hadn't been sated by their lovemaking the day before.

Just one more time. Surely if he made love to her properly, in a bed, one more time, it would finally end the hunger. He knew she wanted him, had seen desire flash in her eyes before she'd turned and ran from the kitchen.

Without being conscious of his own movement, he found himself standing outside the bathroom door. He placed a hand on the doorknob. If it was locked, he'd turn away, go do a series of sit-ups to ease the building pressure. The knob turned easily beneath his grip.

He knew then she wouldn't turn him away, that she wanted him as much as he wanted her. She could have locked the door, kept him out, but she hadn't.

He let go of the knob only long enough to take his clothes off, then he turned it once again, this time entering the steam-filled room.

Through the floral shower curtain he could just barely make out the shape of her, the dark silhouette increasing his desire. When he pulled the shower curtain aside, she didn't jump in surprise, nor did she flinch beneath the intensity of his gaze.

Soap lather clung to her shoulders and dripped down her torso. Her hair was slicked back away from her face, her eyelashes spiked with wetness. She looked beautiful.

"Hank." It wasn't a protest, nor was it a verbal caress, it was simply acceptance.

"I thought you might need help scrubbing your back." His voice sounded odd, husky as it bounced off the walls of the tub. He waited, tensed, to see if she'd welcome him or reject him. His throat grew dry as he waited for her reaction, wondering if he would—if he could—stop now.

She reached out and handed him the bar of soap.

It was all the acceptance he needed. He stepped into the tub, beneath the warm spray and took her into his arms. Her skin was slippery and sweet smelling from the soap, and fire blazed in his veins as the tips of her breasts slid back and forth over his chest.

With the water spraying his back and her body caressing his front, he was overwhelmed with pleasure. He fought for control, feeling like an eager teen experiencing his first foray into lovemaking. And if he wasn't careful, like an inexperienced teen, he'd spend himself before ever actually committing the act.

He stepped back from her and ducked his head beneath the water, then gasped as she placed her mouth against his chest, kissing him with tormenting thoroughness. He wanted her to stop. He wanted her never to stop.

"Oh, Colette," he moaned. Once again he grabbed her to him and captured her wicked lips with his own. His hands ran down the length of her back and cupped the curves of her buttocks, pulling her against him with another moan.

He was no longer sure whether the moans were hers or his own. He was lost in a maelstrom of sensation, emotion so deep, he no longer could tell where she left off and he began. The entire world had narrowed and compressed, becoming only this moment and this woman.

Not wanting to finish what they had begun in the uncomfortable confines of the tub, Hank picked her up in his arms and stepped out of the bathtub.

"Hank...the water," she said as he started out the bathroom door.

He smiled. "We can shut it off later. The government pays the bills."

It was a very long time before the water was finally turned off.

Chapter Sixteen

Twelve more days. Where before Colette couldn't wait for the days to count down, she now found herself wishing each day would last forever.

No longer able to fool herself, she knew she had fallen in love with Hank. And she couldn't help but believe that Hank had feelings for her, as well. Although he didn't say anything, continued to hold on to his silly rules of no commitment, no promises, Colette saw promises in his eyes each time they made love. She'd tasted unspoken promises on his lips as they kissed. She didn't know exactly what the future held, but she wanted Hank to be a part of hers.

She stretched languidly against the cotton sheets, knowing she should get up, but reluctant to leave the cocoon of the sheets that still held the residual scent of Hank's cologne.

She knew Hank was probably already up. Although he'd remained in her room making love to her into the night, he'd slept alone in the second bedroom. She'd discovered he was a man who required little sleep, but had voracious appetites in all other areas.

She smiled, her body still tingling with remembered sensations of his caresses.

They'd spent the day yesterday playing cards to pass the time. Unsurprisingly, she'd found him to be fiercely competitive. During the card games, he'd relaxed enough to talk, telling her stories of his youth that only deepened her feelings for him. He'd spoken of growing up a wild child who communed with horses and hunted pretend criminals with a wooden gun. He spoke lovingly of his mother, his eyes dark with pain when he talked of her death.

Colette got out of bed, suddenly eager to spend every minute of the day with him. She showered and dressed quickly, then seeing that Brook was still sleeping, she went into the kitchen.

Hank sat at the table, a cup of coffee in front of him. He looked up as she entered. "I spoke to the boss a little while ago. They're sending out a doctor to talk to you this morning."

"A doctor?" She poured herself a cup of coffee and joined him at the table. "To try to get my memory back?"

He nodded and eyed her intently. "Scared?"

"A little." She smiled gratefully as he reached out and touched her hand reassuringly. "I keep thinking there's something bad in my memory…something besides the murder."

He pulled his hand back and looked down into his coffee. "Whatever it is, it's possible you'll know soon." He reared back in his chair, his eyes dark and enigmatic. "Before long this will all be behind you, nothing but a distant memory. You'll go back to your life and find some nice man to marry."

"Hank…"

"Don't, Colette." The front legs of his chair hit the floor and he held up a hand, as if he knew the words of love she wanted to blurt, those that burned to be said. "You know my rules. We've managed to make it through a lot together, and found an enjoyable way to pass the time."

"An enjoyable way to pass the time?" Colette's heart ached. She'd thought…she'd hoped…had she been so mistaken? No, she hadn't imagined the tenderness in his gaze, the love that had flowed from him in unguarded moments.

She narrowed her eyes. "I don't believe that's all it was for you. There's more between us than that. I'm in your heart, Hank."

He smiled, not a pleasant one, his eyes as cold as death. "That's impossible, my sweet little coquette. It's impossible because I don't have a heart." He stood. "I'm going to watch the news." He disappeared into the living room and a moment later the sound of the portable television filled the house.

Colette remained at the table, her heart aching with his words. Funny, even this particular heart pain seemed familiar. Was it possible she'd experienced this same kind of thing with Brook's father? Had she mistaken lust for love and he'd rejected her? Had she been a naive little fool not only with Hank, but with another man, as well?

She drew in a weary breath. Hopefully she'd have all the answers soon. Hopefully the doctor would be able to retrieve not only the memories the prosecution needed to put away Collier, but also the personal memories she needed to know.

She was working on her second cup of coffee when Hank stuck his head through the doorway. "The doctor is here," he said.

Fear mingled with anticipation. She stood and smoothed her hands down the side of her sweatpants, nervous, scared...anxious of the answers she might receive, not only about the crime, but about the kind of woman she was. Taking a deep breath, she left the kitchen.

The doctor was a burly man with glasses that couldn't hide his piercing, cold blue eyes. He shook Colette's hand, introducing himself as Dr. Wallace, then turned and looked at Hank. "Perhaps you could get a breath of fresh air or take a walk. A patient generally relaxes more easily if it's only the two of us working together." Hank hesitated and Dr. Wallace smiled. "I'm a cop first, a therapist second." He patted a bulge beneath his coat jacket. "She'll be fine with me."

Hank hesitated a long moment, then nodded and disappeared out the front door. Dr. Wallace turned to Colette and smiled, a gesture that did nothing to alleviate the cold harshness of his eyes. "Now, my dear, if you'll have a seat right there on the sofa, we'll get started."

Colette sank down onto the sofa, her heart thudding with anxiety. "Are you going to hypnotize me?"

"No, my dear." Dr. Wallace eased down into the chair across from where she sat. "At least not right now. For the moment we're just going to talk." He crossed his legs and pulled a small notebook and pen from his breast pocket. "Now, tell me any memories you have about working at Cameron Collier's law firm.''

"I don't have any."

Dr. Wallace frowned at her. "Close your eyes and think for a moment…the memories are there in your head, all you have to do is retrieve them.''

Dutifully Colette closed her eyes, wanting desperately to remember something, anything. She frowned, searching, digging, trying to pierce the black shroud that fogged her mind. Nothing. She opened her eyes. "I'm sorry. I don't remember anything. But I've had some dreams," she offered.

"Tell me," he demanded.

It didn't take long for her to relay what little information her recurring dream contained. "I know it's not much," she finished.

"You wouldn't be faking this bout of amnesia in an effort not to testify, would you?"

"No." Colette laughed uneasily. "If only I were everything would be much easier. I want to testify, I want to do whatever I can to get Collier behind bars, but I can't tell what I don't remember."

"And beyond your dream, you don't remember hearing a conversation between Collier and another man?"

"No."

"And you don't remember being chased down the hallways of the law offices?"

"No."

"Ask the lady if she remembers cutting me."

The voice came from the kitchen doorway. Colette whirled around to see Bob Sanderson standing there. And in the instant of seeing him here, where he didn't belong, Colette's memories whirled, her brain tilted and all her memories locked into place.

It had been Bob's voice she'd heard in Collier's office. It had been Bob who'd chased her down the hallway. Bob was Collier's hit man.

Colette jerked back around to face the doctor, seeking help. To her horror, the doctor tucked his notebook and pen back in his pocket and stood. "I'll just leave you two old friends to get reacquainted," he said, then without a backward glance, he left the house.

HANK WALKED down the sidewalk, the sun warm on his back, his thoughts filled with Colette. All along he'd known he was playing with fire, loving her in bed, attempting to distance himself from her when out of bed.

It had been the same before she'd run, before she'd lost her memories. He'd found himself getting too deeply involved with her. Damn her for crawling beneath his defenses, for making him forget his own rules, for making him remember the promise of hope, the joy of love.

In any case, it didn't matter. Once the doctor helped her get back her memory, she'd remember everything. Not only would she remember the murder, the identity of the hit man, but also the fact that he'd turned his back on her when she'd needed him most. She'd remember she hated him.

It was better that way. He kicked at a stone and watched it skitter across the sidewalk and into the street. Better she hate him than know the truth; that he loved her and was too afraid to do anything about it.

As he came to the intersection that would carry him into the next block, he turned and started back the way he'd come. He wondered how long the doctor would be. Funny, he thought, over the years he'd talked to every psychiatrist the department had on staff, but he couldn't remember ever hearing anyone mention a Dr. Wallace.

A bad feeling rose in his stomach, an instinctive knot of knowledge that screamed something was wrong. He should have never left the house, should never have left her alone with the doctor. Dammit. He'd been in such a hurry to leave because of the personal tension between him and Colette, he'd made a stupid, rookie mistake.

He quickened his pace back to the house, each step causing an increase of tension. When he was two houses away, he broke into a run, all his instincts shouting danger.

It's probably nothing, he tried to assure himself. Just because he'd never personally heard of Dr. Wallace wasn't cause for undue alarm. Still, his instincts refused to quiet beneath the calm rationale.

His bad feeling increased when he reached the house and discovered all the draperies tightly drawn, making it impossible for him to see what transpired inside.

Maybe they closed them to allow Colette no distractions. Maybe a dark room was necessary for whatever methods Dr. Wallace was using as therapy. All the maybes his mind could conjure didn't still his frantic-beating heart, the bad taste in his mouth that told him something was horribly wrong.

He crept around to the back of the house. Peeking into the window, he saw nothing in the kitchen to arouse any suspicion. He tested the back door and found it locked, just as it had been when he'd left the house. Moving farther down the back of the house, he came to the window of the bedroom where Colette had been sleeping. Peering inside, he saw Brook, asleep in the crib. Again intellect fought with instinct. Nothing looked wrong, but Hank felt wrong.

He leaned against the side of the house and pulled his gun from the top of his boot. Now what? He could burst through the front door, gun drawn and hopefully if something was amiss, he'd get a jump on the situation. The worse that could happen would be that he'd disrupt the doctor's work and scare Colette with his unnecessary heroics.

Or, he could play stupid, get back inside and assess the situation coolly and calmly. He replaced the gun in his boot top, then walked up to the front door and turned the knob, surprised to find it locked.

"Colette? Open the door."

There was a moment of silence. "Hank, we aren't finished yet." Colette's voice drifted through the wooden door.

"That's all right. I'll go into one of the bedrooms. Just let me in, it's hot out here."

Again his words were met with pregnant silence, then the soft click of the door being unlocked. Colette opened the door, her eyes wide with some emotion Hank couldn't decipher. "Hank…" She was jerked aside and Hank found himself facing the barrel of a gun.

"Well, well. Looks like old home week. Hank, come on in and join us. Colette and I have been reminiscing about our past." He motioned Hank inside and to the sofa, then shoved Colette down next to Hank.

"It was him," Colette said to Hank. "He's the one I heard in Collier's office. I remember. I remember it all." Her eyes were wide with terror. "I heard their conversation, talking about the death of the councilman. When I turned to leave, I knocked a book off the desk. He...he chased me, but I got away."

"But I found you again." Bob eased himself down in the chair facing them, the gun never wavering. "I found you in Las Vegas."

She nodded, seemingly dazed with the memory. "You chased me through a casino."

"And when I caught you, you did this to me." He stroked the length of the scar on his cheek.

"I had a key in my hand...my room key. The blood. There was so much blood. That's when I lost it. That's what stole my memories...all that blood." She closed her eyes, her face paper white.

Hank's fingers itched to pull his gun, but he stifled the impulse, knowing if he wasn't quick enough Bob would manage to get a shot at Colette. Patience, he told himself, hoping the right opportunity would present itself to get both himself and Colette out of this mess.

"So, you're the one who pushed Colette down that root cellar at the ranch," Hank said.

Bob nodded. "She wasn't supposed to be found."

"And you pushed me off the butte," Colette added.

The gunman frowned. "That wasn't me. Maybe you've got more enemies than you know about at the ranch. All I know is you've been one pain in Mr. Collier's behind."

"And you're going to do Collier's dirty work," Hank returned. "Collier never gets his hands dirty. He always hires big, stupid bozos like you."

Bob laughed. "You think you can rile me by calling me stupid? Get me angry so I make a mistake?" He laughed again. "I'm not doing this for Collier." He pointed the gun at Colette's forehead as his other hand crept up to touch his scar. "This one is just for me. Bang!"

Colette jumped, Hank swore and Bob laughed harder. His laughter died and his gaze grew hard. "Well, this little walk down memory lane has been nice, but it's time to finish this." He stood. "What I have in mind is a murder/suicide scene. Hank here kills Colette, then overwhelmed with grief, kills himself."

"Nobody will believe that," Hank scoffed. His heart pounded frantically as he tried to figure how to get to Bob before Bob got to Colette. As long as Bob held the gun firmly trained on Colette, Hank couldn't take any chances.

"Ultimately I don't care what anyone believes. As long as both of you are dead, nobody can point a finger at me or Mr. Collier. Now, let's go slowly into the bedroom. If you cooperate, I'll even let you kiss each other goodbye."

Knowing no perfect opportunity was going to present itself, as Hank stood he grabbed the gun from his boot. As he shot, he threw himself in front of Colette.

He had the satisfaction of watching Bob sprawl to the floor before Hank became aware of a searing, burning pain in his chest. He heard Colette scream as he crumpled to the floor.

"Hank, oh, God…Hank." Colette fell to her knees by his side.

"Call 9-1-1," he whispered, fighting the blackness of unconsciousness, knowing if he gave in to it, he'd never wake up.

Colette scrambled to the phone and dialed the emergency number. As she screamed into the receiver, Hank raised his head to see how badly he'd been hit. Bad. Blood seeped far too quickly from the wound in his upper chest. If medical attention didn't happen quickly, he feared he would bleed to death.

Colette hung up the receiver and crawled back over to him. "Hang on, Hank. Help is on the way."

Again darkness danced at the edges of his vision, beckoning him into the dark void where he wouldn't feel the pain. He fought it, breathing shallow, fiery breaths as his lifeblood continued to drain. "Colette, you have to help me." He closed his eyes, finding the act of speech exhausting.

"What should I do? Tell me what to do."

He opened his eyes and looked at her, saw the tears that sparkled on her lashes, the fear that trembled her lips. "Get a towel or something. You need to stanch the bleeding."

She left him and was back in a moment, a bath towel in hand. As she leaned over him to position the towel on the wound, he saw that her face was void of all color. "So much blood..." she murmured faintly. She swayed as if fighting a faint.

"I'll do it," he said, knowing how the sight of blood affected her. He tried to raise his hand to place it on the towel.

"No." She inhaled a tremulous breath. "I'll do it." She seemed to draw from a source of strength he didn't know she possessed. Placing her hands on the towel, she gazed into his eyes. "You saved my life."

He forced a smile. "That's my job."

"You're Brook's father." Tears splashed on her cheeks. It wasn't a question and he didn't answer. "You lied when you told me I was pregnant before overhearing Collier. You're Brook's father and you didn't want her. You didn't want me. That's why I ran from you."

Sirens wailed in the distance, signaling their approach. Hank closed his eyes once again, not wanting to see the pain reflected in her eyes. "I never made any promises. You said you expected nothing from me. You promised you understood the rules."

"It's a promise I can't keep." Her voice was thick with tears. "Damn you, Hank. I love you."

"I'm sorry," he breathed softly, then gave in to the darkness that beckoned.

Chapter Seventeen

For weeks Colette had prayed to get her memories back, now she wished she'd lose them once again. She was glad she had the memories to help put away Collier, although they were no longer as necessary as they had been.

Bob was dead and Dr. Wallace had been arrested and was singing enough songs to help put bars around Cameron Collier for the rest of his life.

The trial was set to begin the next day, then Colette would be free to return to Cheyenne. Free to go back to her life with only haunting memories of love and a fatherless child to show for the experiences she'd been through.

She walked over to the window of the lush tenth-floor hotel room. She peered outside, wishing the bright afternoon sunshine could warm the chill around her heart.

"Ma'am, would you move away from the window?" the baby-faced policeman said.

Colette flushed. "I'm sorry. I forgot." She let the drapery fall back over the window. She'd been instructed to stay away from the windows, the officers fearing her making a target of herself for a sniper's bullet. They were taking no further chances with her less than twenty-four hours to go before the trial.

''I think I'll go lie down for a little while,'' she said, more to herself than anyone in particular.

The officer nodded, then returned his attention to his paperback book. Colette went into the bedroom and sank down on the bed. Grabbing a magazine and stretching out on top of the bedspread, she tried to shove away thoughts of Hank.

The past eleven days were a blur of hotel rooms and strange faces. They'd moved her every day to a new location, another hotel room with a different set of officers each time.

She hadn't seen Hank since he'd been taken away in the back of an ambulance, although she'd heard reports on his progress. He'd come through a surgery fine and as of yesterday was out of intensive care. He'd live without scars, without any lingering after-effects despite his ordeal.

Funny, he was the one who'd taken the bullet, but she felt the pain as if she'd been shot. Her heart would carry scars for a long time to come, the scars of loving a man who refused to love her back.

Tears burned in her eyes as she replayed the time she'd shared with Hank. From the very beginning something had connected between the two of them. Within two weeks of her being in his custody, they'd made love, unable to fight the intense attraction they shared. Their lovemaking had brought an intimacy to their relationship that Colette had apparently mistaken for love.

She'd been such a fool. She'd actually anticipated

he'd be happy when she discovered herself pregnant. But he hadn't been happy. He'd been angry, and it had been his anger that had caused her to run.

After stealing all the money he had in his wallet, she'd caught a flight to Las Vegas, certain she could stay hidden in the surreal world of glitter and gambling. And for several months she had stayed hidden...until Bob Sanderson had spotted her.

She'd managed to get away from him, but the horror of cutting his face, seeing his blood, had driven everything else out of her mind.

Brook cried, awakening from her nap, and Colette got up and approached the playpen. Brook immediately waved her hands and legs, as if happy to see her mom.

''Oh, sweet baby.'' Colette bent and picked her up, the cuddly warmth of the child assuaging some of her heartache. She carried Brook back to her bed and placed her on her back.

Studying the little girl's features, Colette was amazed she hadn't seen Hank's genetic stamp before. Now she couldn't look at Brook without seeing Hank in the raven hair that covered her scalp and the dark eyes that peered at her so intently. Even the shape of Brook's lips reflected her father's genes...a father who didn't intend to be a part of his daughter's life.

Damn Hank Cooper. For the first time since she'd gotten her memories back, a flare of anger surged. He'd been so adamant, so self-righteous in reminding her that he hadn't made any promises.

But he had...each time he took her in his arms he'd made a promise; each time he'd made love to her, she'd felt his promise.

Angrily, she wiped a tear off her cheek. Hank was the loser in all of this. He'd miss all the beautiful moments of raising a child. He'd miss all the love Colette could have given him, a lifetime of love and commitment.

"Ms. Connor?" The baby-faced officer stuck his head in her doorway. "We just got word that Cameron Collier killed himself."

"What?" Colette scrambled off the bed and faced him. "When? How..."

"We don't have all the details, but from what we heard his lawyer found him at his home. He hung himself, left a note that he'd rather die than spend a day behind bars." The officer grinned widely. "Looks like you're off the hook, Ms. Connor. You can go back home and forget you ever heard about Cameron Collier."

Home. Back to the ranch with her sisters and no fear of retribution or revenge. Yes, at the ranch maybe she'd forget about Hank. Beneath the blue Wyoming skies maybe her heart would begin the healing process.

Within two hours the powers that be had arranged a ticket for a flight back to Cheyenne, and a secretary to take Colette and Brook to the airport.

"I'll bet you're glad this is all over." The secretary, Amanda Rowen, smiled at Colette as they pulled out of the hotel parking lot.

"Yes." But it wasn't over...not really. Colette realized she couldn't return home until she said goodbye to Hank. She needed closure. "Would you mind taking me by the hospital where Hank Cooper is? I'll just be a minute, but I'd really like to tell him thank you.''

Amanda checked her watch. "Sure, we've got time and the hospital is right on the way.''

As the southern California scenery flashed by, Colette knew she'd be happy if she never visited here again. For her, California would never evoke memories of sunny days and sandy beaches. It would always be the place where her heart had been broken. Too many memories, the good ones as painful as the bad.

It took them only minutes to arrive at the hospital. Amanda sat in the waiting room while Colette, carrying Brook, went to Hank's room.

Hank dwarfed the hospital bed, looking too fit, too vital, for a man who'd been so recently shot. His gaze was focused out the window, away from where she stood. She paused just inside the doorway and took a moment to drink in his features, impress them in her mind, knowing her memories would be all of him she'd carry back to Cheyenne, her memories and his child.

"Hi," she said, her voice husky with suppressed emotion.

He turned and looked at her, as always his gaze dark, giving nothing away of his emotions. "I figured you'd be on your way back home by now.''

"I am...I just stopped to say goodbye before going to the airport.''

"Goodbye," he said, and turned his head away from her.

Anger swept through Colette, rich and full, momentarily muting any pain. "That's it?" She walked

over to the side of his bed and stared at him in disbelief. "That's all you have to say to me after everything we've shared?"

He turned back to look at her. "What should I say?
I'm glad your ordeal is over. With Collier dead you
no longer have anything to worry about." He winced
and pushed a button that caused the head of the bed
to rise. "I never made any promises."

"If you believe that, you're a fool," Colette exclaimed. She bit the inside of her mouth, trying to
maintain control and not allow emotions to overwhelm her. "Hank, you didn't have to mouth words
to make a promise. It was in your eyes, in your kiss."

"You mistook passion for promise," he countered,
his gaze not quite reaching hers.

"I don't think so." She moved closer to the side
of his bed and shifted Brook from one arm to the
other. "Are you telling me Brook was conceived in
lust...not love? Can you honestly look me in the eyes
and tell me you don't love me?"

As Colette said the words, she knew this was why
she'd had to see Hank before she left. She had to
know if her memories of love were true, or if the love
she'd felt from him had only been a fantasy...the
need of a little girl wishing for a prince beneath a
twisted tree.

For a long moment his gaze held hers, and in his
eyes she saw the answer. Euphoric joy swept through
her as she recognized love. "I knew it," she breathed
softly. "You do love me."

"Colette, it doesn't matter what I feel for you. I
intend to live my life alone, without commitment."

His eyes darkened, a whisper of a new emotion deep in their depths.

Colette's joy faded, replaced by a piercing ache. "You're afraid," she said in surprise. "You took a bullet for me, risked your life to keep me safe, but you're afraid to love me."

He turned his head and stared toward the window, as if wishing himself away from the hospital, away from her. Seconds ticked by…tense seconds filled with unspoken emotion and unfulfilled dreams. He finally moved, reaching into the drawer next to the bed. He pulled out a small book and threw it on the bed. "Take it. It's a savings account for Brook. I was going to send it to you, but you might as well take it now."

His words chilled her. "I don't want it," Colette replied, a renewed burst of anger sweeping through her. "She doesn't need your money, and I won't let you salvage your conscience by taking your money." She reached into her blouse pocket and pulled out the gambling chip that had rested against her heart. For a moment she held it tight, remembering. The night he'd given it to her he'd said she was his good luck charm. That had also been the first night they'd made love. She tossed it to him. "Now I guess we're even."

Although there were a million things Colette could say about what Brook did need from him, Colette refused to use her daughter as a bargaining tool to try to make him change his mind.

She walked to the door, feeling dead inside.

"Colette?" She paused at the doorway and looked

back at him. "I never promised." He said it as if it somehow gave him absolution.

She sighed wearily. "You can tell yourself that a million times, Hank. But you did promise. You promised with your eyes and with your kisses. Every time you took me in your arms, you made a promise. Promises don't have to be spoken aloud, and sometimes it's the unspoken ones that hurt the most when they're broken."

"I'm sorry," he said, his eyes dark orbs of pain.

"Oh, don't feel sorry for me." She raised her chin and straightened her back. "I'll be fine. I still have my dreams, my hopes. Even though I love you with all my heart and soul, I won't be like you. I won't let my dreams of happily-ever-after die like you did." She hugged Brook closer against her heart. "Hank, fate is giving you a second chance for happiness." Once again her voice was hoarse, filled with tears and broken dreams. "You're a fool for turning your back on it."

She turned and left the room, hoping, praying he'd call out to her, stop her from walking out of his life. But he didn't. And in his silence, Colette's heart broke in two and she knew she'd lied to him. He had stolen her dreams for happily-ever-after, for she couldn't imagine loving another man as she loved Hank.

"It's all right," she said softly to her daughter, who stared up at her with Hank's dark eyes. "We'll be okay. At the ranch you'll be surrounded by love. And maybe…just maybe, at home I'll be able to forget Hank."

FORGETTING HANK was the most difficult thing Colette had ever tried to do. As the days passed into weeks, thoughts of him still intruded into her days, continued to haunt her with dreams of bittersweet love mingled with heartache.

The twilight bathed the landscape in golden hues as she walked toward the dragon tree. Brook gurgled and cooed in the carrier as if pleased to be out in the fresh air.

Life at the ranch continued to be a daily financial struggle, but everyone had been in high spirits since Colette and Brook's return. Although her sisters had grilled her about the crime, the return of her memories, and Cameron Collier's suicide, they had steered clear of the subject of Hank, as if knowing Colette's heart was too badly bruised to want to talk about him.

She'd left the house after supper, wanting to watch the splendor of the sunset in solitude.

When she reached the dragon tree, she spread out the blanket she'd brought along, then placed Brook in the center and sat beside her.

The sky overhead was a lustrous blend of colors as dusk reached out fingers to claim the blue sky. The air was filled with the sounds of the ranch getting ready for the coming of night...sounds that rang of home. Home. If home is where the heart is...where is my home? Colette wondered. Certainly her heart wasn't here.

Her heart was with a man who'd been strong enough to protect her, but too afraid to commit to her. Her heart was with a man whose dark eyes possessed the power to warm her throughout, whose callused hands could make her body sing.

At least she had Brook. Even though the pregnancy had been unplanned, Colette was grateful for the baby who unmistakably bore Hank's genetic stamp. At least she'd always have this little piece of him.

Funny, she hadn't been able to cry. In the two weeks she'd been back at the ranch, not one tear had fallen. Her heartache was far too deep for mere tears.

She leaned over and rubbed Brook's cheek, laughing as the little girl kicked her feet and waved her hands in excitement. "I'll make you love him," she said to her daughter. "Somehow I'll make you understand that your daddy is a good man, that he was just afraid to love again."

She straightened as in the distance an unfamiliar car pulled up in front of the ranch house. A man got out of the driver's seat and Colette's heart began an irregular beat.

What was he doing here? What could he want? Dear God, she didn't want to see him again. She wished desperately she could hate him.

He looked around, then, spying her, started in her direction. The gasping, dying sun overhead gleamed off his black hair, making it shine with a dark lustre. His strides were long and purposeful, his posture rigid with determination.

Colette stood, hating the way the sight of him filled her with longing, brought all the memories of their time together to the forefront of her mind.

Was it business that had brought him back? Loose ends on the Collier matter? Surely that was the only thing that would bring him to see her again.

"Hi," he said when he reached her.

"What are you doing here?" She was pleased her

tone was harsh. She didn't want him to know how the mere sight of him made the ache inside her intensify.

He shoved his hands into his pocket and rocked back on his heels. "I've come about the job."

She frowned in confusion. "The job? What job?"

"You mentioned that when you got back home there would be a position here for a horse-breaking bodyguard."

She wrapped her arms around herself and stared off into the distance. "The position is no longer open."

"What about the position of husband and father?"

She whipped back around to look at him, her heart racing. "Husband and father?" She eyed him narrowly, then sank to sit on the blanket, her legs suddenly wobbly. "What are you talking about?"

He sat next to her, bringing with him the evocative scent that Colette would always associate distinctly with him. "I'm talking about promises, and happily-ever-afters."

"That's not the song you were singing last time I saw you." She hung on to her anger, needing it to shield her heart from another hurt. She pulled her knees to her chest and wrapped her arms around them, trying to maintain her self-protective anger.

"You're right," he agreed easily. "I was damned and determined when I saw you in the hospital that it would be the last time I saw you and Brook." He smiled down at the baby, and in the tender smile, the first stirring of hope blossomed in Colette's heart.

"Then why are you here?" she asked, her voice tremulous with suppressed emotion.

"It's a funny thing what a bullet in the chest can do for a man. Makes him examine choices he's made in his life, nurse regrets those choices might have made." He frowned, his gaze distant. "Lying there, I realized that I had no regrets, that if I had it to do all over again I would fall in love with Rebecca, marry her, even knowing the pain of loss that was to come."

"She must have been a very special woman," Colette replied softly.

"She was…and the baby she carried."

"Oh…" This new bit of information pierced whatever anger Colette had been trying to maintain. Her heart ached for this man who'd lost a wife, a baby and his dreams all in one tragic moment. For the first time she recognized the depth of his reluctance to bare his heart again. "Oh, Hank, I'm so sorry," she whispered.

He nodded and continued. "But they're gone, and despite my best intentions to not get involved ever again, I find myself in love with another special woman." His gaze captured hers, an inferno of emotions flaming in his eyes. "I'd have come here sooner, but a reaction to some medication kept me hospitalized until late last night. Colette, I thought I could let you walk away from me, thought I didn't care that you and Brook would make a life without me. God help me, I was wrong."

"Oh, Hank." Colette flew into his arms, a sob escaping from her as his arms enfolded her close.

"Colette…" He cupped her face in his palms. "I told you once I never make promises, but I'm going to make one now. If you marry me, I promise I'll do everything I can to be that prince you wanted. I'll spend every day of my life giving you the kind of happily-ever-after you deserve.''

"Hank, all you have to promise is to love me. That's all I need for my happily-ever-after.''

"I do. I love you, Colette. I love our baby, and I want to spend the rest of my life loving you.'' He stood and pulled her to her feet, then kissed her. His kiss was filled with promise, with hopes and dreams.

As the kiss ended, Colette looked upward, where the boughs of the dragon tree were silhouetted against the blaze of the sunset. The promise of a sweet, clear night. Life was filled with promise.

She remembered three little girls playing here, each vowing to find a prince and live happily ever after. With his dark, unruly hair and dusty blue jeans, Hank looked more rogue than prince, but in his eyes she saw her future...a future of forever love.

Epilogue

"Oh, Colette. You look beautiful." Abby dabbed at her eyes as she looked at her sister. Colette stood in the center of her bedroom, her two sisters sitting on the edge of her bed.

"Like a fairy princess," Belinda agreed, her eyes also suspiciously shiny.

Colette twirled around, loving the way the silk wedding gown billowed with her movement, then reached out to embrace each of her sisters. "I can't believe this is happening. I can't believe it's my wedding day."

"You'd better believe it," Abby said with a laugh. "We have a lawnful of people outside and a wedding cake the size of New Jersey. Somebody better be getting married today."

A knock fell on the door. "Mom, the wagon's ready." Cody's voice radiated with excitement. "Bulldog says it's time to get this show on the road."

Abby opened the door to admit her son. Cody danced in, his miniature white tuxedo decorated with smudges of Wyoming dust. "Oh, Cody, you're already dirty," Abby exclaimed in dismay.

"Mom, cowboys don't stay clean," Cody replied, making the three women laugh.

"It's okay," Colette said, ruffling Cody's hair. "I think you look perfect."

Abby looked at her watch. "Bulldog is right. It's time to get this show on the road." She picked up Brook, who was clad in a ruffled pale pink dress, and handed her to Belinda. "You take the kids and go on to the wagon. We'll be right out."

Belinda nodded. With a final kiss on Colette's cheek, she left the room, leaving Abby and Colette alone.

"I feel like since Mama's not here and I'm the eldest, I should say something wonderful and wise but I'm too filled with happiness for you to be able to think straight," Abby said.

Colette hugged her sister. "I don't know what I'd ever do without you and Belinda. I'm so glad you don't mind Hank and me making our home here at the ranch."

"I wouldn't have it any other way," Abby replied. "This ranch is our home...and there's plenty of room for all of us here." She released Colette and wiped her eyes once again. "I'm just so grateful the Collier mess is behind you and you can live the rest of your life without being afraid."

Colette frowned. "Sometimes I wonder, though. Bob Sanderson says he didn't push me off that butte, but there are times I'm positive I was pushed." She shrugged. "And then there are times I'm not so sure. In any case...you're right. It's all behind me."

"And now it's time to get you married to that handsome hunk of yours." Abby took her hand and together they left Colette's bedroom and went outside where a flower-bedecked wagon awaited them.

In the distance, Colette could see the people sitting in folding chairs around the dragon tree. As the wagon carried her closer, she saw Hank. Tall and proud, he stood beneath the tree in front of the preacher, his gaze warming her despite the distance.

It had seemed right that they marry beneath the dragon tree. Colette had explained to Hank that the tree was a place for vows. It had been here that Colette and her sisters had vowed their love and devotion to each other, here that they had played out their dreams of handsome princes and happily-ever-afters.

As the wagon pulled to a halt, Hank stepped forward and helped Colette down, his hand warm, his gaze loving.

As their friends and neighbors looked on and with the dragon tree shielding them from the heat of the sun, Hank and Colette spoke the vows to unite them as husband and wife.

"I now pronounce you husband and wife," the preacher said, then smiled at Hank. "And you can kiss the bride."

"With pleasure." As Hank's lips claimed hers, she tasted the sweet promise of love, knew her fantasy had come true and together they would live happily ever after.

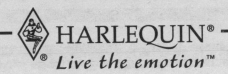

HARLEQUIN®
INTRIGUE®

BREATHTAKING ROMANTIC SUSPENSE

Shared dangers and passions lead to electrifying
romance and heart-stopping suspense!

Every month, you'll meet six new heroes
who are guaranteed to make your spine tingle
and your pulse pound. With them you'll enter
into the exciting world of Harlequin Intrigue—
where your life is on the line
and so is your heart!

THAT'S INTRIGUE—
ROMANTIC SUSPENSE
AT ITS BEST!

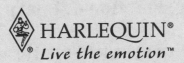

HARLEQUIN®
Live the emotion™

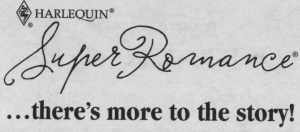
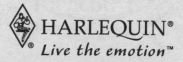

Harlequin® Historical
Historical Romantic Adventure!

Imagine a time of chivalrous knights and unconventional ladies, roguish rakes and impetuous heiresses, rugged cowboys and spirited frontierswomen— these rich and vivid tales will capture your imagination!

Harlequin Historical . . . they're too good to miss!